The (Extra)ordinary Life of Jimmie Mayfield

By

Troy Young

Copyright © 2020 by Troy Young

ISBN: 978-1-7770603-8-1

Contents

Chapter 1

The cigarette blazed to life as Jimmie Mayfield touched the lighter's flame to it. He inhaled deeply, chasing it with a spoon of Frosted Flakes and topping it off with a swig of Diet Coke. The potent cocktail of nicotine, sugar and caffeine combined in his system, leaving him euphoric. He leaned back on the rusty metal clamshell chair on his dilapidated patio. The hot Florida sun beat down as he took a long drag on his cigarette. He put his feet up on the table and closed his eyes. This was the life.

Jimmie rubbed his hands through his luxurious hair. He kept it long in the back and short up front, and with his signature mutton chops, he resembled a 1970s southern rock god lounging in front of the mouldering trailer he shared with his mother. A less than fresh tank top hung from his slight frame, a thin layer of buttery fat under his skin a testament to his fast-food diet and lack of exercise regime.

Jimmie ate the sugared flakes, wondering if he should go back inside and grab something to read. He was a voracious reader. But his moment of contentedness overwhelmed his desire for reading materials. Or perhaps it was laziness? He couldn't decide and spent no mental energy trying to figure out which it was.

His morning routine was sacrosanct for him; it was the closest thing to a religious ritual in his life. But an obnoxious voice shattered his routine.

"Hey Limp Dick, you up?"

Jimmie was both happy and disturbed by the source of this disruption; the voice belonged to his best friend, Rob Peele.

"Don't call me that. I don't have a limp dick."

"Oh, I guess you knew I was coming, did you? Fag," said Rob. Short and stocky, his blond hair in retreat, Rob kept it buzzed and hidden under a "Fairfield Marina" hat, his place of employment. He had a love of boats and wanted to be around them, even if he couldn't stand their owners. He wore a faded t-shirt of his beloved Tampa Bay Buccaneers.

"Your toxic masculinity is intruding on my calm existence. Please refrain from using derogatory terms to describe people. There is nothing wrong with being gay, so don't imply there is. Why are you here?"

Rob ignored the admonishment. "They got me working a later shift. Ryan dropped me off, and Clint's picking me up here."

Rob depended upon the kindness of others since his driver's licence got suspended. A few months back, he had been at home drinking alone when he ran dry. He drove to the liquor store, but in his state, Rob didn't just drive there; he drove through the store's front doors. Unfazed by the carnage, he got out to shop for more booze. Rob calmly waited to pay for his purchases as the police arrived. He was lucky not to be in jail and had since cut back on his drinking.

"Hey."

Rob's younger brother Ryan rounded the corner of the trailer. "I gotta go. Just saying hi." Ryan left.

"When is Clint coming to get you?" Jimmie said to Rob.

"Why, are you in a rush to rid yourself of me?"

"Curious minds want to know."

"I shall bless you with my company for the next half an hour. Try to contain yourself."

"Is this what being blessed feels like? I expected being blessed would feel more awe-inspiring."

"Ha, ha. You're a funny man. You missed your calling."

Jimmie's face twisted into a grimace. Not because of Rob's comment, but because of the man who further disrupted his moments of peace. Jerry.

"Look at this idiot," said Jimmie. "What the hell does he do around here? I only ever see him fighting with that ancient lawnmower. Look around, Rob. The flower beds are a mess, the paint's faded and cracked, and the goddamn party room is so full of crap that no one can use it. This park has gone to hell since Jerry took over as the park manager."

"How long has he been here?" They gazed at Jerry as he bent over to start the lawnmower, his bright red shorts hiked up way too high and clinging to his nether regions. "Gah," said Rob as he averted his eyes.

"Too goddamn long. Mom and I moved in here in 1994, and I can't remember if he was here then or showed up after us. I think before." Jerry pulled too hard on the cord of the lawnmower, and it slipped out of his hand. The momentum of his pull caused Jerry to fall unceremoniously onto his backside. He crawled back to his feet and took off the faded green visor he always wore, and hit the mower with it. Seized by a thought, Jerry bent over and unscrewed the gas cap and shook his head. Noticing Jimmie and Rob watching him, he turned towards them.

"I forgot to fill'er up with gas," he said with his always present half-smile and a shrug. He pushed the ancient machine out of sight.

"I'm not a violent person, but some days I want to smack that stupid look off Jerry's face," said Jimmie.

"Give him a break. Jerry's not that bad. He's always nice to me when I visit the park."

"He's nice to everyone. I think it's a front to cover up his gross incompetence."

"Whatever, dude. You're grumpy today."

"I don't enjoy being interrupted during my morning me time."

"Morning me time? Your entire day is me time. What were you going to do today? Sit around this dump doing nothing followed by nothing? I mean Jesus, a man can only jerk off three or four times before he's shooting dust. Then what would you do for the next seven hours, huh? How am I the responsible one? You need to get a job."

"Wow, you come over here unannounced and disrupt me in my Fortress of Solitude to insult me? Nice. Not how I pictured my day going, thank you very much." While Rob's attack stung him, he could not contradict the statement.

"Tough love, brother. Someone has to do it. Your mom coddles you. She ain't never going to say 'get off your ass and get a job.'"

"I've had a job. Lots of jobs."

"Yeah, and you can't keep them for more than a few weeks," smirked Rob.

"I have had a series of unfortunate incidents. I had a great job at Pretzel Joe's."

"Jesus, that was thirteen years ago! It was part-time at the Port Charlotte Mall!"

"I had that dishwashing gig at Captain Fernando's Seafood Emporium."

"That place where the old lady who owned it came up behind you to slide your night's tips into your front pocket? I'm sure you loved it!"

"Mrs. Cline was a lovely lady. Her actions were completely innocent."

"Uh-huh, sure it was. So why did you leave there?"

"Mrs. Cline retired and turned the day-to-day running over to her son. He was a real dick. And I got sick of coming home smelling of seafood."

"Had nothing to do with the fact that instead of taking the garbage to the dumpster, you lobbed it off the balcony, caught the edge of the dumpster and filled his Corvette convertible with old lobster bodies?"

"That may have played a slight role, yeah. Who parks their convertible next to a dumpster?"

"Loser."

"My problem is bad luck, not my lack of desire to be employed. I made poor choices at the two I have mentioned. I did not know they would close or that my inability to hit a basket would be problematic. What about my job at McDonalds?"

Rob snorted. "One from this decade. I wondered when you'd bring up McDonalds. Go on."

"You know full well why I left McDonalds. They created an unsafe work environment. The pervert of an assistant manager sexually harassed me. He exposed his penis to me."

"Ha! You walked in on him in the employee bathroom because he forgot to lock the door!"

"That may be, but he took his sweet time turning back around to the urinal to hide it."

"You stunned him, and he wondered why you were standing there staring at his dick!"

"They made me uncomfortable. I couldn't stay there."

"Bullshit. You wanted out of that job. Why? Because you think these jobs are beneath you. I put in an honest day's work. Sure, I may not be perfect, but I manage on my own. You sit here and let your mom take care of you when she has trouble taking care of herself these days." Rob paused for a few seconds to compose himself. "Where is she? I want to say hi."

"She's over at Chester's again."

"She's been over there a lot, huh? Getting serious?"

"It's been getting something. What that is, I'm not sure. It's good for her. She needed someone, right? We all need someone. And it leaves me alone in the trailer, which is nice."

"If you enjoy being alone, ever consider getting a place of your own?"

"And leave Pleasant Meadows? Nah, I like it here."

"Your trailer is a dump."

"It has seen better days, that's for sure. The floor's gone spongy; the humidity is killing it. It's past its useful life. I'm sure if some authority were to inspect it, they'd condemn it. But it's still home."

"It's like the 1970s threw up inside it."

"It's a temple to the period's faux-luxury. This trailer was top of the line in 1973," Jimmie smirked. "And the horde of other people's cast-offs my mom has collected over the years hasn't helped."

"It's like the crap left at the end of the day at the world's saddest yard sale."

The sounds of people arguing interrupted their conversation. "McCarthy's are at it again," said Jimmie. "All they do is fight and have loud make-up sex."

Rob laughed. "What were you planning to do today anyway?"

Jimmie shrugged. "Maybe I'll go to the library; I have books I need to return."

"You and your books. I guess reading is better than doing absolutely nothing."

"I like to read. And since mom lost her job, we haven't had a TV in the trailer. Her compensation pays the rent on the spot and keeps us fed, but not much else."

"How is her eyesight?"

"Her glaucoma is not getting worse, but she can't see worth shit. The weed is helping. The sad thing is there is a laser surgery that could prevent any further vision loss, but we can't afford it."

Rob shook his head. "Listen, Jimmie, you need to help your mom out more. You should get a job."

"We back to that again?"

"You need a spark. Your mom can't keep looking after your sorry ass. You need to look after yourself."

"You know what? Screw you."

Rob sighed. "Listen, man, I didn't intend to come over and beat on you, but..."

"You're doing a good job, regardless of your intentions," bristled Jimmie.

"I'm only doing it because you need it. You were always the dreamer of our group. But you are as lazy as shit."

Rob made him seethe. Like Rob was so successful, working as a gas jockey at a marina, his brother spending his day spraying used bowling shoes, while... Jimmie's anger abated a glimmer when he remembered what Rob had said about Jimmie thinking menial jobs were beneath him. Did he really believe that?

"Your mom needs your help. You can't live this way forever."

He almost let Rob in on his big secret. He kept his plans to himself until they came to fruition, except for telling his mom, for reasons he could not explain to himself. Occasionally, on a day when his liver didn't work at peak efficiency and did not sufficiently filter out his nicotine/caffeine/sugar cocktail, he would do something out of character. And once he embarked on one of these journeys, he would approach them with a tenacity and focus which surprised everyone, even himself. He had started a new plan months ago and now waited to know his fate.

Unsure if he'd passed, there was no point sharing it with Rob. He was afraid that by saying it out loud, he'd jinx it or sound unrealistic. He sighed and kept it to himself. A billboard had acted as a catalyst this time, and he was now in a six to eight week waiting period. One of these days, he'd get all he deserved.

"Listen, I'm sorry I went off on you. Things have been shitty for me for the past few months, what with Claire taking off and my incident at the liquor store. It's my stupid fault, I know, and I kinda fucked up, but I sit here, and I see you kinda fucking up your life even worse than I am with mine. Get your head out of your ass and do something useful. At least leave the goddamn park today for more than the library."

At that moment, the sound of an ooga horn split the air. Clint had arrived.

Clint Lewis was a former defensive lineman for their high school football team and a large, intimidating man. He had been popular in high school, but Jimmie, Rob and Ryan were his closest friends (much to everyone's surprise, none more than Jimmie, Rob and Ryan). Clint had gone off for a year of college on a football scholarship to a small school in Alabama. The transition to college football had been a challenge; while gifted, he did well at high school level ball with little effort. But college-level ball took dedication and commitment, something he wasn't interested in doing. He gave more energy to the classes he enrolled in than football, but they didn't give him a scholarship for his academics. So, after a year of sitting on the bench, they revoked his scholarship, and he returned to his home in Englewood.

Clint had two real passions in life: fixing cars and chasing women. He turned his talents at one into a decent career, working at Delvecchio's Chrysler-Jeep-Ram as a mechanic. His abilities at the other allowed him to become, as he labelled himself, the 'Don Juan of Englewood'.

"Hey boys, what's new?" said Clint, with the lazy drawl he used. He threw his large frame into one of the empty chairs, causing it to strain. Clint had let himself go in these post-football years, but, with effort, he could return to his playing condition.

"Ah, I've been giving him the gears," said Rob.

"What are you two lovebirds arguing about now? You're always on him for something."

"Rob says I need to get a job and do something with my life."

"Well, he ain't wrong," chuckled Clint. "What have you done since that guy caught you peeking at his pecker at Mickey D's?"

Rob laughed as Jimmie went red-faced. "I wasn't peeking at nothing! I'm the victim here! You guys need to validate what I'm feeling."

"Holy shit, son," said Clint. "Validate what you're feeling? Have you been reading those damn self-help books at the library again? Or your mom's trashy magazines?"

"I'll have you know my mom doesn't buy magazines anymore on account of her eye troubles. I wasn't peeking at nobody's nothing."

"As much as I'm enjoying this, I will be late for work," said Rob. "Why don't you come with us? I mean, do more today than sitting around jerking off."

"Yeah, why not? You're right; I had no plans. You being here has screwed up my curated routine."

"Oh yeah, the routine. Can't mess with the routine," said Clint, as he heaved himself up out of the chair. He slapped a big meaty hand on Rob's shoulder and stuck his other hand in front of Rob's face. "You smell that?"

Rob screwed up his face as he tried to pull back, but Clint held his hand fast in place. "What the hell is that?"

"Oh, you know what, boy. Got a case of the stinky fingers."

"Ugh, why do you do this, dude?"

"Ah, you love it, and you know it. You live vicariously through me. The four of us combined have the average sex life of any group of four men in their late 20s," said Clint. "Unfortunately for the three of you, I'm the only one getting any!"

"I get my fair share!" said Rob.

9

"I think our definition of fair differs," said Clint. "You been with anyone since Claire dumped your sorry ass?"

Rob looked at his feet. "No. I'm still trying to work past it."

"You read those same magazines that Jimmie is? You got to get over it. We are men, and we need sex. Get that sex, boy!"

"Some people prefer companionship to empty sex, Clint," said Jimmie.

"And how's that working for you, huh? You've had a more successful working career than sex life."

"Whatever. We can't all be you."

"You're right," said Clint. "It takes a special man to reach my lofty heights. You guys don't have it in you to be as awesome as me."

"This has been a weird start to my day—first Jimmie, now you. Let's go. I don't want to be late."

"It's fifteen minutes away, dude. Don't get your panties in a twist," said Clint.

"Let me get my flip flops," said Jimmie

"Don't take all day. Rob here doesn't want to be late!" Clint gave Rob a wink as he headed to where he parked his Jeep.

Jimmie picked up the dishes off the patio table, slid open the screen door with his foot, and bounced across the floor, heading to the sink. He grabbed his sunglasses, slipped on his Adidas flip flops and hurried out the door to catch up to his friends.

Chapter 2

Jimmie hustled out to Rob and Clint sitting in Clint's Jeep Wrangler. Rob had shotgun, Jimmie in the back. He loved being in the back. Not only did he feel he was on an adventure, but when they hit the open road, and the wind began to fluff his hair, he felt alive.

Clint fired up the engine, and the radio roared to life. Jimmie sat back and let the wind work its magic on his hair. Rob and Clint were going on about something in the front, but he wasn't paying any attention to them. He enjoyed the moment.

They drove along the highway, through the sprawl of the low-rise buildings, parking lots and palm trees, typical southwest Florida on full display. A billboard caught Jimmie's eye. The sign which acted as his current inspiration.

A man who represented success to Jimmie gazed down upon him. His slicked-back luxurious silver hair, earnest face displaying what appeared to be a genuine concern. Bright, caring eyes on a face with a slight jowl, his right hand reaching out to you, looking to pat you on the arm reassuringly or pull you in for a much-needed embrace. His dark navy suit contrasted with his white dress shirt and blue tie. The body under the suit leaned towards a soft roundness; he dined well but didn't exercise. His accoutrements spoke to

11

wealth: the diamond ring glittering on his pinky finger, the Rolex watch peeking out of the sleeve of his suit, the jaunty silk pocket square. And the message written in bold gold lettering on the blue background said:

Injured? Immigration Problems?
DUI? Divorce? Accused of a Crime? Hurricane Damage?
Put your trust in the Monroe Group.
Four generations of lawyers helping the people of Southwest Florida for over 50 years.
Free Consultations. We don't get paid unless you win.
The Monroe Group: Fighting for you!

Here was a great man—a man of the people. Jimmie wanted to emulate him. He daydreamed of being such a man when Rob's voice brought him back to reality.

"Hey! Have you not been listening to us? Clint's asking if you want to see the WWE in Sarasota?"

"I haven't watched the WWE since mom got rid of cable two years ago, so I wouldn't know the storylines. I prefer the local independent wrestling shows anyway. Besides, I see two obstacles to that happening. One, how am I going to afford a ticket? And two, that means going to Sarasota. I have no wish to visit the city of snobbery; if I haven't gone there in the past twenty-nine years, I'm not about to now."

Clint snorted. "It's thirty miles from here? You've never visited Sarasota?"

"Had no reason to as everything I need is right here. Why would I want to visit a bunch of douchebags? I also see no reason to head inland either. Florida is blessed with over a thousand miles of coastline and great beaches; there isn't a compelling reason to venture away from the coast unless it's visiting Orlando, I suppose. Never been an amusement park kind of guy, but I guess if that's your thing, go for it."

"Why are you talking about our beaches when you hate the beach!" laughed Rob.

"Hate might be too strong a word. I dislike many aspects of the beach. It's hard to walk on, the sand gets into your nooks and crannies, it's hot, and it's crowded, and never as fun as you think it will be."

"The beach has ladies in bikinis," said Clint.

"There is that. I said I dislike many aspects of the beach, not all aspects. Besides, I can see that from the boardwalk without having to venture out onto the sand."

"Standing on the boardwalk like some creep?" said Clint.

"Unlike being a creep on the beach? Like you?" said Rob.

"The difference between me and a creep is a creep lurks and watches. I engage. Jimmie and you lurk."

"You don't want to head inland, and you don't like the beach. Are you happy anywhere?" asked Rob.

"I like it here in Englewood. Things are familiar, and I have a comfort zone. We have everything we need right here. Why go anywhere else?"

"So, you've been nowhere?" Rob queried.

"I went to Fort Myers once. Too big and congested for my liking."

"That's sixty-five miles south of here," said Clint. "You have been nowhere then."

"Saw no reason to go anywhere else."

"Wow."

Clint pulled into the parking lot at the Fairfield Marina. The dichotomy of Englewood on full display amid the myriad of vehicles. Parts of it were like Pleasant Meadows, but parts catered to those with wealth. Cadillacs, Mercedes, Audis, Range Rovers and the odd Porsche or Ferrari filled the marina's parking lot. The boats lining the docks were worth more than the average person could make in a lifetime. A restaurant on-site with a dockside bar attached sported a beach theme: seashell ornamentation, palm-thatched roof, nautical implements and charts. A few employees cleaned the place up, adorned in Hawaiian style shirts and white shorts, getting ready for the lunchtime crowd.

"I got to check-in. Be right back," said Rob.

Jimmie looked around at the boats. "This is the life, huh? These people have made it."

"Meh. Rob hates these people. He loves boats and being around boats but hates the owners. You say Sarasota is filled with snobs, but this is ok?"

"These people are our snobs."

"These people don't give a shit about you or me. I see people like this at work. We're here to serve them, nothing else."

"It's the American dream to be successful."

"One man's dream is another man's nightmare. Hold on, check out this one."

Clint nodded towards an attractive older woman. Her once blond hair had faded to a soft grey. She wore a pair of black yoga pants with matching teal running shoes and t-shirt. A white visor and large round Gucci sunglasses completed her look. She stood on the dock, enjoying a leisurely coffee.

"That one's fine," said Clint.

"She's a little old, don't you think?"

"Don't use the term 'old'; it's disrespectful. She has matured, like a fine wine. Let me tell you about her."

"Oh, I'd love to hear your story."

"That woman had a middle-class upbringing. She went off to university and joined a sorority. Then she met a boy. Some young professional, someone with his career planned out. A future doctor, lawyer or architect. She got married right out of school. She had a job, a teacher or a salesperson in a high-end retail boutique. This was while her husband completed his extra schooling. Soon after he starts his career, she gets pregnant—the first of three kids. Never goes back to work. She's a full-time mom and devoted wife to Mr. Man. Joined the local PTA, was active in her church. The kids grew up. Her house is empty. She's in a book club, plays tennis a couple of times a week, yoga in the morning, goes for a jog, meets the girls for lunch. All her life, she's been doting on others, doing nothing for her. Now the kids don't need her, her husband is a success and doesn't need her help,

14

and they've settled into a comfortable place of thirty or more years of marriage. She loves her family, but she's bored. There is a fire in her. Just a spark for now. With the right application of oxygen, she could be a raging inferno." Clint winked. "I should say hello."

"All that from looking at her, huh? What gave it away? The visor?"

"Heh. Most people have tells, like in poker. You'd be surprised what you can learn by watching people."

"You go away to university, take an intro to psych class, and now you're Sigmund Freud."

Clint shrugged. "Years of experience. I know what I know."

"You think all women want to sleep with you?"

"Not all. Just the smart ones."

Rob returned. "I'm checked in. Thanks for the ride, Clint."

"No worries. But hey, before I go, help us out here. We were talking about that woman."

"Who? Mrs. Monroe?"

"If that's what she's called. Tell us about her."

"Her husband is a big shot lawyer. The dickhead with those radio and TV commercials and those stupid billboards everywhere."

Jimmie perked up. "Luther Monroe? Of the Monroe Group? That's his wife?"

"That's the dickhead. She's okay, though. I mean, for being one of the jerks who own boats here."

"Hmm, her husband is a lawyer, is he?" said Clint with mock sincerity, giving Jimmie a wide-eyed, sideways glance while making an air checkmark. "Tell me, do they have any kids?"

"Yeah. Their brood of douchebags visits all the time. I think they have three. The oldest douchebag just bought a boat of his own, one of the modest ones."

"Hmm, three kids, you say." Clint made another checkmark in the air. "And what does she do for fun?"

15

"An awful lot of questions, Sherlock. Am I on trial? I see her going for a run in the morning. She's often having lunch with a gaggle of hens over at the restaurant. This seems to me to be an unhealthy obsession."

"Clint's bragging he figured out most of that by looking at her. You've confirmed it for him. Now he will be even more insufferable. Don't encourage him."

"Ah, yes. Mr. College Man knows everything now."

Clint made a third air checkmark. "Now I have to confirm the fire inside her. Stand back, fellas, as I introduce a little oxygen." Clint walked towards her.

"What the hell is he talking about?" asked Rob.

"He thinks she's a bored housewife who needs to sleep with a guy like him."

"Yeah, good luck with that," scoffed Rob. "These people run in their own circles. They barely notice people like us."

Clint stood near her, not paying attention, gazing at the boats and the water. Mrs. Monroe glanced at him. Her glance lingered longer than Rob and Jimmie anticipated.

Clint pretended to notice her for the first time. "Morning, ma'am," he drawled. "Looks to be a beautiful day today."

She smiled. "Many beautiful days here by the water."

Clint smiled back. "I see the beauty right in front of me. Enjoy yourself today. Just make sure you put on sunscreen; you don't want the sun to damage your flawless skin." Clint strolled back towards them, throwing a wink their way. Mrs. Monroe's eyes followed him.

"What the hell just happened?" asked Rob.

"Sometimes on the hunt, you go in guns blazing. Other times you got to lay the bait and sit back and be patient. Guns blazing would scare her off. No, she needed the bait. And she's sniffing it right now. I just needed to introduce a little oxygen."

"But, you said nothing."

"Didn't need to. Just had to get close, let her breathe in my scent, my musk. Break the ice, pay her a compliment and get out. You don't linger. She'll think about me all day."

"Right," said Jimmie.

"It's like the Seinfeld episode, boys. I've got the Kavorka, the lure of the animal. It makes this easy. That and confidence. You guys will never understand, so sit back and watch a master at work."

"You're incorrigible," said Jimmie, as he sniffed himself and tried to sniff Clint without him noticing. Both Rob and Clint laughed at him.

"I have to go, boys. Going to see if I can't dip my root before work." He laughed and walked away.

Rob shook his head. "He's full of shit. No way he gets as much as he says."

"I try not to think about Clint and his sexual prowess."

"It's hard not to since it's all he goes on about."

"It is his favourite topic, for sure."

"I have to get to work. What are you going to do now?"

"I don't know. Maybe walk to the library and read. Get my lunch." He had a thought. "Hey, since you were giving me grief about getting a job, is there anything I could do here?"

Rob looked at him. "Listen, man, I love you in a non-gay sort of way, but no way in hell will I help you get a job here. I like this gig, see? And if you work here, you'll screw it up for me."

Jimmie was hurt. "How am I going to screw it up for you?"

"If you mess up here, it'll look bad on me since I recommended you. Given your history, it's only a matter of time before you say something stupid to one of the owners or accuse someone of molesting you or other stupid shit. But even if you didn't, you're an energy leach. It's a goddamn gift of how you can do nothing at all. You make me want to do nothing. I can't do that here; I have to hustle at work. I'll end up spending my time hanging out with you, and soon we'll be sitting around doing nothing, and both end up fired. So, no, I won't help you."

"You're an ass. I will not mess things up. We won't get fired."

"History shows you are not a good risk. Sorry boyo, but that's the way of it."

"Rob! Get over here! The Joneses want gas for their boat." shouted the dock manager.

"See? You're getting me in shit just being here. See you tonight. Want to go to Gator's?"

"Why do you want to hang out with me since I'm such a loser and cause you nothing but grief? But what else do I got?" He shrugged. "If I don't go to Gator's, I'll be sitting at home doing nothing. Oh, I forgot, I'm good at that."

"Shut up and stop having a pity party for yourself. Use that brain of yours for something worthwhile. I got to go." Rob sighed. "I'll even buy you a beer because I was an ass today."

"You mean an even bigger ass than normal?"

"Hey, don't push it. See you around, butt-munch." Rob hurried off, leaving him standing at the edge of the parking lot alone.

Chapter 3

"Jimmie, I want you to spend time with Chester. To get to know him," said Dolores.

When Chester kept coming by, Jimmie knew his mom expected him and Chester to interact. *That's what normal people do, right?*

He had done fine without a father in his life. There was one faded picture of the family hanging in the living room, a Sears Portrait Studios family photo where everyone looks awkward. Jimmie was six in the picture; his dad died six months later of pancreatic cancer. It devastated Dolores; Danny Mayfield was a good man, father, and husband. Jimmie had vague memories of his father. He remembered the music. And dancing. If his mom had been with anyone else since his father died, she had kept it from him.

"Chester's a good man. He treats me well. He's honest and caring. My special men need to get along."

"I'm not saying Chester's not those things, Mom, but I'm not sure what we have in common. What will we say to each other?"

"No one expects you to become buddies. And I don't expect miracles overnight. But it has to start somewhere. Chester and I talked it over; he's as nervous as you, but he is at his trailer right now waiting for you."

"I'm not nervous. This feels forced. Things need to happen on their own."

Dolores scoffed. "We've been an item for three months, hun. The two of you get edgy and end up grunting like cavemen at one another. It's because I'm there. The only way forward is to force you to spend time together. Alone."

"I need to prepare myself for this. You've just sprung it on me. Give me two weeks to ruminate before I have to do it."

Dolores snapped. "I've asked you to do this. Now I'm ordering you. This is no longer a request. If you expect any allowance, you will march right out of this trailer Jimmie Mayfield and visit Chester. Do not return until you've talked." Dolores took a long drag from the joint smouldering in her ashtray.

Defeated, Jimmie agreed. "Yes, Mom. I'll visit Chester. And not because you ordered me. I love you. He's important to you. It's not easy to do, though."

"It's easier to rip the Band-Aid off than to pull it slow." She took another drag and butted out the rest. "It's tough. But thank you. It means a great deal to me." She gave him a big hug.

He patted her on the back. "So, right now?"

Dolores broke the embrace and gave him a slap on the arm. "Yes, right now. Go on, git."

Grabbing the bottle of Diet Coke out of the fridge and checking to make sure he had his cigarettes on him, he headed out the door. The late afternoon sun blazed away; his fast-food lunch sat heavy in his belly, exasperating his sense of discomfort at this task. He removed the cap and took a big swig out of the half-empty bottle. He lingered until the caffeine did its work and lit a cigarette. He alternated between drags on the smoke and swigs from the bottle as he walked across the park, remembering when Chester moved here.

#

Chester moving into the park had caused a stir among the residents. People didn't leave the park; most couldn't afford to. The residents owned their trailers but rented the space off Bill Leblanc. Bill's dad built the park in the 1950s. Its many amenities made Pleasant Meadows, well, pleasant. But Bill took over the park from his dad, and things became less pleasant. Residents from when Bill's dad owned it remembered the way it used to be.

So, it was a big event when someone new came to the park. Most plots were occupied, but there were a few available. The first sign a new resident was moving in was when a brand-new trailer arrived in two pieces and assembled on site. Jimmie and several residents watched them unload it.

"Hey, Jerry," asked Eleanor, one of the older tenants. "What's going on?"

"Bill's rented this space to a fella," said Jerry. "He told me to come and show them where to put it."

"That's a nice trailer," said Mike, another resident. "Look at those floors. It will be the best one in the park. Why bring something nice to this dump?"

"Just what we need," Jimmie said. "Some rich asshole wants to slum it with us common folk."

A few days later, the new owner moved in. Jimmie and Dolores were sitting out on the patio, both smoking their chosen substance, when Mike sauntered by. "Hey, have you heard? The new guy's here. He's black."

"So?" said Jimmie. "Why should that matter?"

"What, that he's moved in or he's black?" said Mike confused. "It's been a long time since somebody moved into the park. We should have a barbecue or something."

"We should," said Dolores. "We used to have park gatherings all the time. Why did we stop?"

"Because the place is deteriorating around us. The pool hasn't been usable in what, fifteen years? Then they closed the party room and left us with nothing," snorted Jimmie.

"Hush now. Be good for us to get together and welcome him. Who will organize it?" asked Dolores.

21

Mike shrugged. "I'll ask Jerry. Maybe there's a fund we could use to help pay for it?"

As Mike walked away, Jimmie scoffed. "No sense asking Jerry. Man can't do anything right."

Dolores had heard his rants on Jerry. "Oh, leave him alone. There is nothing wrong with Jerry."

"Have you seen this place? It's going to hell. Ever see Jerry with a can of paint? Or fixing things? The only thing I see him do is fiddle with the lawnmower. I bet he's been pocketing the money he gets to keep this place tidy. I should write to the owner and tell him what Jerry's doing to the place."

"If I thought you'd do it, I'd worry about poor Jerry," she snapped back. "Are you coming to the barbecue?"

"Why?"

"To be neighbourly."

"No. If I run into him, I'll say hi."

A few days later, they held a small gathering. Dolores went while Jimmie stayed home and moped around the trailer. He lay on their old couch when his mother returned.

"Well, Chester is such a gentleman," said Dolores. "And his trailer is gorgeous. He's retired and wanted a nice little community he could call his own. A place he could meet people. He's worked all his life and only ever had an apartment. The hassle of a house on a piece of land didn't appeal to him. This was a nice compromise."

"He chose here?"

"What's wrong with here?"

"Nothing. We've been here for a long time. But I can't imagine anyone coming in off the street and thinking 'here. Here is where I want to be'."

"Well, he was shocked," admitted Dolores. "The cheap rent is what attracted him, but the pictures he saw of the place were from its glory days."

"Not sure how bright it is, moving into a place without having seen it."

"You're smart, but you have to stop thinking people are stupid," chided Dolores. "I've invited him and the McCarthy's over to play cards tomorrow night."

"That's fine," he said. It was Friday, and he'd be heading to Gator's.

"I don't want you running off until you've met him," said Dolores. Jimmie rolled his eyes.

The next night Chester showed up early, a bottle of wine and flowers for the hostess. "Oh, you didn't have to do that," said Dolores, blushing.

"My momma raised me proper," said Chester, stealing a quick glance at the trailer's tired appearance. "When you go to visit someone, you bring a gift. And I wanted to thank you for doing your best to welcome me. I hoped to settle in a community like this."

Dolores continued to blush as she took the flowers to put them into a vase. "Chester, this is my son Jimmie. Jimmie, get up off the couch and welcome Chester."

He got up and sauntered over, his hands in his pockets. He nodded his head at Chester. "Hey."

"Hey yourself." Chester nodded back.

Jimmie glanced over at the clock. He hoped Rob would get here soon.

"So, what do you do?" asked Chester, making small talk.

"I've got something in the works."

"I see," said Chester. He stared at Jimmie for a few moments and said. "Dolores, can I help you with anything? Anything at all?"

"Aren't you a dear," she said with a smile. "No, you relax and talk to Jimmie."

"Ok," said Chester.

Jimmie stood there, staring. "I'm going out soon. My friend is picking me up."

"Good to know," said Chester.

"Yeah."

They stood there for what seemed like hours. Rob knocked on the door a split second before he slid it open and broke the awkward scene. "Jimmie! Mrs. M!"

"Oh, hello, Rob," said Dolores, coming in from the kitchen. "Rob, meet Chester. He's new to the park."

"Hello," said Rob presenting his hand to Chester. Chester gave it a hearty shake.

"What are you guys doing tonight?" asked Chester.

"We're headed to the church to serve food to the less fortunate like we always do on Friday nights," said Rob with a wink to Jimmie.

Dolores laughed. "Yeah, right. And that's why Jimmie comes home smelling like a brewery."

"I try to lead a chaste and pure life," Rob said, sweeping off his hat and putting his hand over his heart. "But your son is a bad influence."

Dolores laughed again. "Oh, you always make me laugh, Rob. How's that girlfriend of yours? Claire, right?"

"She's fine."

"You planning to make an honest woman out of her?"

"I've been saving a bit of money…"

"Congratulations are in order then."

"When she says yes. Who knows what could happen?"

"Before you ask that question, you should have an idea of what the answer will be."

"I have an idea." Rob smiled a huge smile.

"Well, I am happy for you. Now find a girl for Jimmie…"

"Mom!" Jimmie exclaimed.

"Oh, shush. A mother can dream, can't she?"

"We should go. It was nice meeting you, Chester. Always good to see you, Mrs. M."

"Say hi to your mom and dad, and to Ryan," said Dolores.

"Let's go," said Jimmie, ushering Rob out the door.

#

The (Extra)ordinary Life of Jimmie Mayfield

Jimmie finished his cigarette and his drink as he approached Chester's trailer. He dropped the butt into the bottle, let out a loud burp, put the cap on and dropped the bottle into the garbage can outside. Taking a deep breath to calm his nerves, he walked up to the door and knocked.

Chester opened the door as if he had been waiting behind it. He looked uneasy and grimaced as their eyes locked.

"Jimmie," he said with a brief nod.

"Chester."

They stood there for an awkward few moments until Chester stepped back into the trailer. "I guess I should invite you in."

"Unless you want us to stand here all day."

"Well, come in. Come in," said Chester as he gestured into the trailer.

Comfortable looking leather furniture and a large TV dominated the living room. The cool kiss of the air-conditioning caressed his skin; their own air conditioner had broken years ago, and they never replaced it. He understood why his mother spent so much time here.

Chester opened the door on his stainless-steel fridge. "Your mother tells me you like Diet Coke. That you drink a lot. I never touch the stuff, but I got some for you. Would you like a can?"

"I prefer it in bottles, but yes, I'll take a can, thank you."

Chester took a tall glass from the cupboard and placed it and an unopened can on the table opposite from where he stood. "Sit. You want me to add something a little stronger to it? I might need something a little stronger," he chuckled.

Jimmie sat down. He popped open the can and poured it into the glass, the bubbles threatening to foam up over the lip. He sat there fixating on the effervescent popping of the carbonation.

"Thanks," he said as Chester sat opposite him. Jimmie continued to stare at the glass. Chester stared at his hands. The only sounds penetrating the silence were the popping of the bubbles, the tick-tock of a clock from somewhere within the trailer and the sounds of the McCarthy's arguing in the distance.

"Your mom wants us to get to know each other."

"Yep."

"She's a hell of a woman," said Chester.

"Yep."

"I intend to see her for a long time. I'm not planning on going anywhere. So, I guess you and I have to try. For her sake."

"Yep."

"You always this loquacious?"

"Sorry, Chester. I don't know you. It's been mom and me for a long time. It's never been easy for us, but these last three years have been even tougher. You've helped, I admit. She's happier lately, so you deserve credit for that. But she sprung this on me, and I'm having issues processing this, ok?"

Chester nodded. "I understand." He paused. "I get what you mean drinking soda out of a can compared to a bottle. They taste different. It tastes best coming out of a glass bottle; gets flat too fast out of a plastic bottle."

"Glass bottles are the best if you can find them, although the soda often has a syrupy taste."

"That it does." They both nodded again and looked away. The tick-tock of the clock returned.

Chester cleared his throat and got up from the table. "I need something stronger. You sure you don't want me to add some rum?"

Jimmie hated rum. "Yes, please."

Chester pulled a bottle of spiced rum from the cupboard and grabbed a high ball glass. He poured a swig into Jimmie's glass before pouring two fingers worth into his own. Then he returned to the refrigerator and got a handful of ice cubes, which he dropped into his rum with a splash. "Bottoms up," he said as he took a sip.

Jimmie stifled a shudder as the alcohol burned his throat.

26

"I worried when I moved here, would people accept a black man? Few black folks in Englewood."

"Didn't bother me. I don't care what colour someone's skin is."

"Well, thank you for saying that. Lots of folks still do. I find it means less to younger people than it does the old folks. But everyone has been real nice, very welcoming. And I started to worry when your mother and I took up together. Me living here is one thing, but..."

"Gossip happens in insular communities. There is nothing else to occupy them. But they are good people here."

"Yeah, I suppose. I never had much of a place. I was always working, spending my time on the water. I slept at my old place and not much else. When I retired, I wanted someplace that had a community feel. Still, it's taken some getting used to. I'm not used to a life of being idle."

"What did you do?"

"I worked on a commercial fishing boat," said Chester. "I was the captain for the last fifteen years," he added with pride. Chester looked at his hands again, uncomfortable. "And what is it you do?"

"I'm between opportunities."

Chester nodded. "You've been between opportunities since I moved in here."

"That's right."

"I mention it because your mother worries about you and your lack of... opportunities."

"This is an ongoing theme today. Everyone is worried about me and my lack of... opportunity."

"I've not had much experience with this. I mean, I got my first job at ten years of age, picking oranges in an orange grove. The owner let me keep some; I sold them at the side of the road. I always had a hustle going"

"Uh, huh."

"I saved up my orange money, and at fourteen, I bought a car—delivered bread for a bakery. I didn't even have a driver's licence. Drove that car into the ground. Ended up on a fishing boat at eighteen. That's hard work, hauling in those monster fish, gutting them and getting them on ice. Get home after dark, bone-tired, smelling of fish guts. Shower off the stink, throw yourself into bed, get up the next day and start again. Six days a week."

"You're making it sound so romantic."

"Shush, young man. No one expects you to do that. But that's what I did. Every day for forty-five years. And it paid off for me. The guy I worked for see, he retired. I worked harder than anyone else he had on his crew. He made me the captain, trusted me to keep his business going. You know what it's like to carry that kind of responsibility? I worked the boat and crew hard, and we made him a lot of money. He always took care of me.

"He died a few years after that. His daughter ran the business by then, and she kept me on as captain. Continued to look after me. You know what happened when I told them I was retiring?"

"No idea."

"She sold the damn boat! Said they would find no one they could trust like me. She'd diversified the business and only kept the boat because they didn't want to take it from me. Why am I telling you this?"

"You're bragging?"

"Hell, no. I'm telling you to have some responsibility. I worked hard all my life, I bought this trailer with cash, and now I get to enjoy the fruits of my labours and settle down. Never had a steady woman in my life until I met your mom. This is new to me, but damn I see you lazing doing nothing."

"Apparently, I'm good at doing nothing."

"Not something to be proud of, son."

"So, like everyone else in my life today, you're telling me I need to get a job."

"I'm saying you need to have some pride in yourself because if you did, you wouldn't be sitting around doing nothing. When I first saw you, I thought you were doing nothing because you were a retard."

"Hey, don't use that word. It's thoughtless and cruel and categorizes an entire group of people as lesser. You

28

started off this discussion being worried about how people would take the fact you were black when you moved in, and you use words like that."

Chester was taken aback. "Ok, ok, I'm sorry. I didn't mean to offend. Tough for an old guy like me to change the way he talks, and everyone is jumping down us old folks throats these days for talking like we always did. I get it, I guess. You didn't do much, and when I heard you talk, you just grunted; I thought you were slow or something."

"Slow?"

"Yeah, slow. Like you were a reta... like you were dumb. You stood around with your hands in your pockets, saying little. You didn't make an excellent impression."

"Thanks."

"Jesus." Chester picked up his rum and downed it in one shot. "This is not going well. I told Dolores it wouldn't go well. I don't know how to talk to people, especially young people. She assured me you weren't slow or nothing; she said you were smart, just lazy." Chester took a deep breath as Jimmie glared at him. "Lookit, I'm sorry. These things have been playing on my mind. I like your mom and want this to work out with her, which means working it out with you. Someone like you and someone like me, what do we have in common? I wasn't going to say anything; I hoped you'd say more, but when you didn't, it came out."

"I can't believe you thought I was slow."

"You have a look about you. I mean, who wears their hair like that these days?"

"You're not making it better. Don't besmirch my personal style."

"I'm sorry. Sorry. Just... sorry."

The McCarthy's had stopped arguing. That meant they had ten minutes before their make-up sex began. He wanted to be gone before it started.

"Ok, Chester. I will forget the last five minutes, and I suggest you do the same. We'll do this again for my mother's sake. Later," he added, "because I've had enough for now."

"Right."

Jimmie pushed back his chair and got up from the table. "Thank you for the drink, Chester. You have a beautiful home. And thank you for telling me about yourself. But I'm going."

"I understand."

He headed for the door and paused before he opened it. Without turning, he said: "We have something in common."

"What's that?"

"We both care about my mother. And we both care enough to put ourselves back in this awkward situation."

"That we do."

"Before we do this again, I'll learn about commercial fishing so I can ask questions. You find out why the word retard is wrong. Our next discussion should be more promising."

"Sure thing, Jim."

"It's Jimmie. Says so on my birth certificate. No one calls me Jim."

"Good to know."

"See you around, Chester."

He opened the door and stepped into the sun.

Chapter 4

Jimmie didn't go home right away. His mom would be interested to know what happened with Chester. He didn't feel like telling her.

He headed to the pool. When Pleasant Meadows opened, the park had a public space with a laundromat, party room and a well-maintained pool. But then came Jerry. The party room was closed to residents and became nothing more than storage for crap Jerry couldn't be bothered to haul away. Only half the washers and dryers in the laundry still worked, but the pool was the worst. It had degenerated into something best avoided. Half filled with brackish water, the odour of the decaying vegetation floating in it kept most people from using the rusting patio furniture. The fact an alligator had moved into the pool unbeknownst to the residents four years ago, discovered when it came out and made a snack of one of Eleanor's Chihuahuas, meant most residents gave the place a wide berth. That's why he headed there.

Seven months had passed since he had his ill-fated job at McDonalds for three shifts. It had been six months before that since he had a job, working for a landscaper. That one lasted less than a week; he wasn't cut out for physical labour. Jimmie had not prepared himself for his future.

He had no idea what he wanted to do when high school ended. His marks weren't bad, but not high enough to receive a scholarship. Formal education beyond high school was not part of his plans. They couldn't afford it, even with student loans. For the first few years after graduation, his mom did well enough to support them both, and she didn't want to push him, figuring he'd come into his own. But since she stopped working, he thought he'd do something to help, but he couldn't find the motivation. Not until seven months ago when he came up with 'The Plan' and enrolled in a school.

He secretly spent that time going to the library and working on his courses. He wrote his final exam five weeks ago, and since then, his daily routine had gone back to being one of limitless lethargy. Should he wait until he received the results or find something in the meantime?

Maybe Rob was right. He looked down on these jobs because he thought he deserved better. He needed to find something.

Back in high school, he had a great job at the mall, and he had his own car, a gold Toyota Corolla. This gave him money in his pocket, freedom to roam and a place he belonged. He sat in one of the chairs, pulled out a cigarette, and found himself thinking about the past.

#

The mall was more vibrant then than today. He arrived right after school to start his shift on a Wednesday. The mall wasn't busy on Wednesdays, so he'd be working alone at Pretzel Joe's.

"It's been slow today," said Mary, the daytime assistant manager, as he arrived. "I prepared a fresh batch of dough for you, so you should be good for the evening. Need anything else?" Mary was maternal; she reminded him of his late grandmother.

"No, I should be fine, thanks."

"Have fun tonight." Mary pulled on her cardigan. She flipped up the counter and exited the store. "I have to go to JC

Penny's and get a dress for my granddaughter. I'll swing by before I leave." She meandered into the sparse crowd of the mall.

Jimmie walked into the back and pulled a hairnet over his mullet. He loved his job. The pay wasn't bad, he got to eat all the pretzels he wanted, and he watched Caroline. Caroline Ward attended high school with him; she worked at the kiosk in front of the pretzel shop. He'd never have had the guts to speak to her at school, but working here put them on equal footing. The first time she ordered a pretzel, it took everything he had to keep his cool. He'd been working here for nine months, and he had asked for his shifts to coincide with hers at the kiosk.

Interacting with her had given him newfound confidence. He could relax around her. He still didn't talk to her at school, but here at the mall, they had something special for those few hours, three days a week.

She hadn't arrived, so he pretended to be busy. Once the after-school crowd showed up, the current pretzel supply would not suffice. Jimmie wanted to wait for Caroline before he made more. He was a magician with the pretzels.

He liked to put on a show as he rolled out and cut the dough. The way he spun the long, thin pretzel dough into the various shapes delighted the customers. They often watched him work. He'd be the centre of attention, at least for five minutes as he made them.

"Hi," said Caroline as she arrived and gave him a wave. She wore a yellow baby doll top over a pair of jean shorts and gladiator sandals. It contrasted with her tanned skin, her bleached blond hair and her bright blue eyes. His heart leapt into his throat, and his knees grew weak. "Hey Caroline," he returned, trying to sound cool, his voice cracking.

"Can I get a soda?"

"Sure!" Pulling off a waxed cup and filling it up from the fountain, he passed her the drink, not charging her as always.

"Thanks," she said, looking at him right in the eyes, cocking her head and wrapped her lips around the straw. Jimmie was oblivious to the fact she knew what she was doing to him.

Jimmie cracked his knuckles and got to work. He finished his twirls and placed the pre-baked pretzels in the oven. In eight short minutes, he'd have some fresh pretzel goodness to serve.

He looked up and saw Joe, the owner, coming towards the store, followed by two guys pushing a large dolly. "Hey, Joe," he said, confused. Joe rarely went to the store.

"Oh, hi, Johnny," he said as he pulled up the counter and held it open for the two guys to enter.

"It's Jimmie."

"Huh? Whatever." Joe turned his back on him and talked to the two guys. "I want everything that isn't nailed down. Start in the back; I'll start here."

The guys moved into the back. Sounds of the refrigerator being opened and large tubs of dough being lifted and thrown onto the dolly could be heard.

"What's going on, Joe?"

"We're closed, kid," said Joe as he opened up the register and started to remove the cash. He stuffed it into a cloth bag, slammed the drawer shut and unplugged it.

"Closed? What do you mean closed?"

"I mean, we're done. I'm getting what we can before the bank gets their hands on it," said Joe, not looking at him. Joe headed over towards the drinks fridge and began to load the contents onto a plastic flat.

"Just like that? Closed?"

"Yep. Shit happens sometimes," said Joe, emptying the fridge.

"What does that mean for me?"

"I don't give a fuck."

"What about my job?"

"You no longer have one."

A guy in the back yelled: "Hey, those pretzels smell awesome. Can we have them?"

"When they're ready. Knock yourself out," Joe yelled back. He glanced at Jimmie and yelled back to his guys, "Leave one for the kid; he looks like he'll cry."

Guffaws erupted. "Sure thing."

"Look, Johnny..."

"Jimmie..."

"Whatever. Fuck. Listen, we don't have all day. We're getting this shit out of here, and then we're coming back for the oven. It's on wheels, right?"

"Yeah."

"Great. When those pretzels are baked, wrap 'em up for the guys and unplug the oven. We need to load it on the truck."

He nodded his head, dumbfounded. "Sure."

"Lookit, kid. It's too bad you're caught up in this. But I'm not the bad guy here. The bank is the bad guy. You can take it up with them." Joe looked at him, sighed, took two diet Snapple Lemonades off the flat and gave them to him. Joe then reached into his wallet, took out a twenty-dollar bill, pressing it into Jimmie's hand. "Here's your severance. You guys done back there?" he growled.

The two guys manoeuvred the cart from the back. "When you're done unloading, come back and help me with the oven and remember to unhook the canisters from the fountain machine."

The oven dinged. The pretzels were ready.

"Quick kid, wrap those up and give them to the boys. And unplug the oven."

Jimmie moved like an automaton. He pulled the pretzels out and slid them into their sleeves. "Thanks, kid," they said, stuffing them into their pockets.

Caroline snapped pictures of the scene playing out in front of her. Someone later posted the photos around the school.

Joe and his guys grabbed what they could and headed out. Jimmie unplugged the oven, turned off the Pretzel Joe's sign and stood there, not knowing what else to do.

35

Joe and his guys came back and grabbed the fountain canisters, the cash register and wheeled the oven away. "See you around, kid."

He stood there in disbelief as a smiling Mary returned, the JC Penny bag clutched in her hand. She stopped, and her eyes widened in disbelief.

"Jimmie... what... oh..."

Her hand went to her mouth, and she began to shake with tears. He awkwardly hugged the old woman while Caroline snapped another picture.

Chapter 5

Rob and Ryan swung by after work to take him to Gator's. The local bar was a curiosity, attracting families and tourists during the day and locals at night. It had a rustic look with a variety of Florida sports team jerseys hanging on the walls.

The retaining pond gave the place its name and made it a hit with the tourists. The pond lay fifteen feet below the old rickety deck and was home to several large alligators. Luckily for the bar, the deck had not given way in the past twenty years, and only one patron was dumb enough to jump into the pond (he got fished out but lost a shoe to a gator's snapping maw).

"Fellas," said Rob. "Today has been a hella stressful day for me. I tore a strip off Jimmie, got yelled at at work, and had an extraordinary number of douchebags and dickheads giving me grief. Time to get my drink on. Boys, let's tear this place up tonight!"

"I'm light on cash," said Jimmie.

"What else is new? I said I owed you one. ONE," Rob stressed, holding up one finger.

"I can cover you," said Ryan.

Rob made a face. "Uh-uh. We shouldn't be enabling him. Everyone enables him. He wants to come out and drink, then he should figure out how to carry his own way."

"You starting on me again?"

"Nope, just preaching the Gospel according to Rob. Let's go."

The music assaulted their ears as they opened up the double doors. Ryan and Jimmie found seats at the bar while Rob made the rounds. "He goes on about getting ripped, but I'm driving, and you can't afford to, and he tells me not to buy you a drink."

"Yeah, an often confusing and contradictory man your brother is."

They caught the bartender's eye, and she came over to them.

"Hey, guys. The usual?"

"Hey, Myrna. You got it. Three Yuenglings, please," said Ryan.

"Make it four," said Clint as he arrived. "Jesus, Myrna, what the hell are you wearing?"

Jimmie inspected her. Myrna Grey had been two years ahead of them in school. He hadn't known her well when they were there, but for the last six years, they'd been regulars at Gator's and got to know her better. She was plain: her nose was too long for her face, and her chin was weak. But she had the most beautiful, bright blue eyes he had ever seen, with a smattering of freckles and strawberry blonde hair. She wore a short black skirt that showed off her shapely legs. He never remembered seeing her in a skirt before and had never noticed her legs. A plunging neckline on her tight black t-shirt showed off her assets, but she looked uncomfortable. Since she didn't have curves to her waist, the whole effect was of a black candy apple on two thin sticks.

"The boss told us we needed to sexy it up. Numbers are going down midweek. Figures if we showed some skin, we'd get more guys in."

"Myrna, sexy and you do not belong in the same sentence. Maybe I could drink enough to make that work, but I'd most likely get alcohol poisoning."

"Fuck you, Clint."

"You wish. Look here," he said, pulling out five one-dollar bills and laying them on the bar. "This here is your tip. For that comment, I'm taking one back." He picked up one bill and put it in his pocket.

"Asshole," said Myrna as she went to get their beers.

"Ah, ah, Myrna. You lost another one," as Clint made a show of taking another bill away. Clint turned towards Jimmie, gave him a wink and gathered up the bills, placing them in a nice pile. He added the two he had taken back to the collection.

"Why do you do that to her? Is this one of your techniques at getting a woman?"

Clint scoffed. "She doesn't like me, never has. No reason to pretend otherwise. So I don't try."

"And why doesn't she like you? You do something to her once?"

"Nah," said Clint. "She doesn't like me because she figured me out a long time ago. No sense uncorking the kavorka for her. She's immune."

"That'll be sixteen dollars. Should I start a tab, or do you want to settle up now?" said Myrna, bringing the beers over, doing her best to ignore Clint.

"Thanks, Myrna, the first round is on me," said Rob, returning. He slapped a twenty on the bar. "Keep the change."

"Cheers fellas," said Rob, handing the beers out to them. "Here's to the kisses we've snatched and vice versa."

The bar started to get busy. Glancing around to see who was here tonight, he noticed men's eyes throughout the bar pivoting towards the front door as Caroline entered.

Still as beautiful as she was in high school, she gave the guys near the door exaggerated hugs and kisses on their cheeks; her hand lingered on their arms as she touched them.

Rob noticed him staring towards her. "Ah, Jesus, will you give it a rest?"

"What?"

"You've been mooning over her for years. It will never happen."

39

"I don't know what you're talking about. I don't moon over her."

"Yes, you do," agreed Ryan.

"You do," said Clint. "Although not sure why. She's not all that. I'd know. I hit it years ago."

"Half the guys in this bar have hit it!" laughed Rob.

"Have you?" asked Clint. Rob blushed. "Yeah, that's what I thought," chuckled Clint as he left them to go mingle.

"She's not like that, Rob. She's... special."

"She's hot. I'll give you that."

"We used to get along when she worked across from me at the mall."

Rob took a swig of his beer. "You're living in the past. You remember the pictures of you plastered around the school?"

"She told me she didn't do it."

"No. She took the pictures," said Ryan.

"And shared them with a hundred people," said Rob. "She might not have copied them and taped them up, but she's the reason everyone saw them."

"You ever talk to her? You don't know what she's like."

Rob shrugged his shoulders. "I know enough not to like her." He got a grin on his face. "I'll be back, fellas." He took off into the crowd, heading towards the digital jukebox, which acted as the sound system.

"What's he up to?" he asked Ryan.

"I don't know, but it can't be good."

They sat there nursing their beers when Roses by Outkast started to play.

"Oh, oh. Why does he want to antagonize her?" said Ryan.

"Oh, he didn't do that, did he?" said Clint coming back. "She figured it out yet?"

While Clint and Ryan were giggling to themselves, Jimmie's face went bright red. He scanned the bar for Rob, but he'd disappeared. People near Caroline were paying attention to the lyrics and chuckling. Then the lyric stating Caroline was the reason for the word bitch played.

By now, Caroline realized people around her were snickering, and she'd heard the bitch line. She looked around fiercely, and her eyes alighted on Ryan, Jimmie and Clint.

"Aw, shit," said Clint. "I'm out. You guys are on your own." Clint faded away.

Caroline came over, anger flashing in her eyes. "You think it's funny, you little creep?" she yelled at Ryan.

"No!"

"Then why are you laughing, you spastic little shit?"

"I don't know! I'm not... I didn't do it," squealed Ryan.

"You didn't. You're too big a pussy to do it. It's probably that stupid brother of yours. You tell him if I see him, I'll gut him like a fish." She glanced over at Jimmie. "Oh, hi, Jimmie." She gave him a brief smile, looked back at Ryan, and cuffed him in the back of the head. "Stay out of my way, freak!"

Caroline left them alone.

Jimmie and Ryan sat in silence for a few minutes, drinking their beer and peeling the labels off of the bottles. "I'm out. I'm going to get another one," said Ryan.

"Uh-uh."

"You going to be mad at Rob when he gets back here?"

"Nope. I'm blameless. Caroline spoke to me and gave me a smile. I'm good," he said as he drained the last of his beer.

"Ok," said Ryan, shaking his head. Raising his hand, he flagged Myrna. "I'll have another, please."

"Sure thing."

She reached into the cooler and grabbed two beers. She placed one in front of Ryan and one in front of Jimmie. "Four dollars Ryan. Jimmie, yours is on me."

"Thanks, but what for?"

41

"You look like you need one. Caroline shouldn't have yelled at you guys. You had nothing to do with that song."

"I got a smile because of it," said Jimmie.

Ryan made eye contact with Myrna out of sight of Jimmie and rolled his eyes.

"Well, maybe you are oblivious to character flaws. And positive character traits," said Myrna, coolly. "Enjoy your beer." She left.

Ryan took a swig of his beer and looked over his left shoulder. His eyes bulged, and beer foamed out of the neck of the bottle as he pulled it away. "Shit. Tonight just keeps getting better."

"What is it?"

"It's Claire."

Jimmie noticed her against the wall, talking to someone he didn't recognize. "I thought she moved to Jacksonville?"

Ryan nodded. "She did. I don't know why she's back here. Don't let Rob see her."

Claire and Rob were together for four years. He decided to ask her to marry him. Rob made reservations at the Gasparilla Inn on Boca Grande, followed by a walk on the beach where he got down on one knee and asked her the question. She looked at him, not speaking for a few minutes, then closed the ring box, handed it back to Rob and said: "No." She left him on the beach, confused and hurt. A week later, she moved to Jacksonville. Rob had not seen or talked to her since. This incident contributed to Rob's DUI; normally more responsible, her leaving had left him in a dark place he still lingered in.

"Hey fellas, did you like the song?" laughed Rob as he came back over to them. "Boy, she looked pissed. Looked good on her." He turned to Ryan. "I saw her smack you. Stupid bitch."

"Hey Rob, we should go," said Ryan.

"Go? Shit, we just got here. I mean, the place is half empty still." His eyes scanned the room and alighted on

Claire. The colour drained from his face. "What is she doing here?"

"I don't know. I just saw her myself. We should go."

"Naw. Naw. Fuck that. This is my bar, my town. She wanted to run off, that's her problem. She doesn't get to come back." He stared in her direction, his voice rising. She must have heard him over the din of the bar because she looked up, and they made eye contact. Her face hardened.

"You hear me, boys?" Rob's voice rose even louder, to where people were looking at him, his face a mask of fury. "She ran away! She left! This is my bar! This is my town! She doesn't get to come back!" His eyes were locked right on hers like laser beams. "YOU DON'T GET TO COME BACK!" he screamed at her.

Everyone now looked at Rob. The talking had stopped. The pulsing sound of the music covered the awkwardness.

Ryan reached out to grab Rob's arm. "Rob..."

"I'm out of here," he said over his shoulder to Ryan. "FUCK YOU!" he screamed in Claire's face as he pushed past, slamming the door to the bar as he exited.

"I gotta go. Claire," said Ryan. "You used to hang here, but seriously? You had to consider you'd run into him."

Claire lowered her eyes, unable to look Ryan in the face. "There was a chance I would run into him, but... I didn't expect this. I should go."

"You might as well stay. Rob ain't coming back in here. Maybe never," said Ryan. He sighed, "You look awesome, by the way. Please, don't do anything else to antagonize him, ok?"

"I didn't intend to antagonize him...I...I... didn't think."

"Yeah," an edge entered Ryan's voice. "I got to go. Jimmie?"

"I'll catch a ride with Clint."

"Right." Ryan left the bar looking for his brother.

Claire looked at him. "Hi. Mind if I sit?"

He liked Claire. She was a good friend, funny, decent and cared for Rob. Jimmie had been at as much a loss as the rest of them when she left him.

"Sure, I guess. Seat's empty."

"Thanks," said Claire as she eased herself onto the barstool. "You won't get in trouble with Rob, will you? Fraternizing with the enemy?"

"Are you the enemy, Claire?"

She sighed. "No, I'm not. Rob might disagree."

"Rob might be glad we talked. Maybe he'll get some answers to the questions he's been pondering."

"He could have tried asking me himself."

"How? You left."

"He knew how to find me. If it was important, he could have followed me."

"Important? He asked you to marry him, Claire!"

"Yeah," she sighed and placed her two hands on the bar in front of her. "I need a drink. You want one?"

"Sure."

"Hey Myrna, whatever he's drinking for him, and I'll have a gin and tonic, please," she said as she started to reach into her purse.

Myrna nodded, grabbed the bottle of gin, upended it into a glass for a few seconds, and topped it off with tonic water. "Good to see you, Claire. You keeping well?"

"As well as expected, yes."

"You up in Jacksonville?"

"That's right. Got a decent job up there. I'm back to visit my parents. Dad's under the weather. I needed to get out of the house and relax. I realize now it was a mistake to come here."

"Yeah. I noticed. You ok?"

Claire gave a quick nod. "I will be."

Myrna handed Jimmie his beer without looking at him and took Claire's money. She left without another word.

"So, how long you back?" asked Jimmie.

"A few days."

"This your first time back since... since, well, since you broke my best friend's heart?"

"No, I've been back twice. I kept a low profile."

"Pity you didn't today."

"Yeah."

The two sat and sipped their drinks in silence.

"Look, I loved Rob. I still love Rob. I hurt him bad, but I never wanted to. It's just..."

"Just what?"

"I started to suspect what he would do. He's terrible at keeping secrets. The Gasparilla Inn? That place is super fancy. He'd never taken me anywhere like that before. It wasn't my birthday, or our dating anniversary or Valentine's Day, so something was up."

"Yeah, he can't keep secrets. Mr. Obvious."

"I started to think about it. We'd been together for four years. It's what people our age in love do. I started to think about settling down with him and starting a family."

"And you couldn't see yourself doing it with him?"

"You've got it wrong. I could see myself with him. I mean, Rob is far from perfect, but he is a good man, and he loved me, and we could have been happy together."

"Sounds like there is a 'but' coming?"

"But," she nodded. "It's this place."

"What, Gators?"

"No, Englewood."

"What's wrong with Englewood?"

"Nothing is wrong with Englewood," began Claire. "I needed to explore what life offered away from here. I wanted to experience things, visit places, push beyond the confines of here. I could be happy here, but I didn't want the sum of my existence to be Englewood."

"Did you tell Rob this?"

"No," admitted Claire. "I didn't. I didn't think it would matter. He was happy. Rob had his dream job, his family, you. He was so comfortable with everything he had here. I didn't see him giving it up."

"He might have. For you."

"He might have. But he might not have. I didn't want him to have to choose. So, I made the choice for him."

"So, you left."

She nodded. "I didn't know what my answer would be, conflicted right until he gave me the ring. I almost said yes. But I couldn't." She wiped away a tear. "I needed to get out. I needed more than Englewood could provide me."

"But you never gave him that choice."

"No, I didn't. I had hoped he might follow me, but when he didn't, I figured I had my answer. I couldn't lure him away from here."

"It might not be too late."

"Yeah, it is."

"You don't know that. You owe it to him to try."

"It's not that simple. I kinda complicated things."

"What? How?"

Claire steeled herself. "I slept with Clint."

"WHAT?"

"It happened after we broke up," she added. "I was never interested in Clint. He's a pig. But the last time I came back to see my parents, I ran into him at the gas station. We got coffee. I was broken up, I'd not gotten over Rob, I felt alone and cut off from everything. Clint and I got to talking, and it seemed Rob didn't care for me anymore. Rob moved on from me."

"You saw how much he's moved on from you tonight."

"Yeah," said Claire, draining her drink. "Believe me, I'm not proud of what I did. But it's happened, and I can't change that now. But Rob wouldn't understand."

"I'm not sure I do."

"Yeah, you do. You're more perceptive than you let on. You're way smarter than most people realize. But Rob wouldn't be able to get over it, and I couldn't go back to him without him knowing. I can't ask him to come with me to Jacksonville under this cloud."

"So that's it then, I guess?"

46

"That's it," she shrugged. "You can't change the past."

Jimmie sat there for a moment. Rob would want to know the reason Claire rejected his proposal, why she had left. But the thing with Clint... he could not tell Rob. Rob would try to kill Clint and fail and be beaten senseless.

"I have a strange question to ask. Feel free not to answer it if you don't want to."

"Ok."

"It's Clint. The way he goes on about things. We think he's full of shit. That he doesn't get as many ladies as he says he does. We're not sure..."

"Whether to believe him?"

"Yeah."

Claire shrugged. "He is a pig. I've known him long enough and seen his tricks. But he has an aura about him that... works. I don't know what it is."

"The lure of the animal."

"What?"

"Nothing. So, how was he?"

"Oh my god. Why are you asking that?"

"We've always been curious."

Claire sat back and crossed her arms. "It is a strange question. But..." she paused. "He's good."

"Really?"

"Yeah. Best I've ever had."

"At least now, I know."

They sat there in awkward silence for a while.

"You had to ask?" asked Claire.

"I did."

"You kinda wish you didn't?"

"Yep."

The awkward silence returned.

"So, enough about me. What's going on with you?"

"Nothing. Same as always."

"You found a job? Last we talked, you'd walked out of that McDonalds gig..."

"Holy Christ, why is my employment status such a concern for people today?"

"Sorry," said Claire. "It's just a thing to ask. I'm curious about what my friends are doing. You've had nothing since then?"

Jimmie itched to tell someone other than his mom what he was up to. He'd always had a cozy relationship with Claire, and it's not like she'd be able to tell anyone. The secret gnawed at him; he'd almost spilled it on a few occasions. He decided to tell her.

"I signed up for a paralegal course. I'm waiting to hear if I've passed."

"A paralegal course? What does a paralegal even do?"

"They help lawyers, organize case files and do legal research. I've always liked to read and discover things. It's a respectable profession," said Jimmie, getting excited. "Paralegals are in demand. It's one of the fastest-growing professions in Florida right now. There are lots of jobs opening up. I applied for financial aid and got a grant the Monroe Group provided. I'm hoping it will help me get a job there."

"The firm with the radio and TV ads? The billboard guy?"

"That's the one."

"Rob says he has a boat at the marina. Says he's a real dickhead."

"Yeah, well, he helps people. Lots of people. I want to help him help people."

Claire touched him on the arm and smiled at him. "You've always had a good heart. And you're smart. I'm sure you'll be a success at this."

"Thanks. I wish I felt so confident. It's a six to eight week waiting period to find out the results. I'm at week five right now. This is what I did with my days."

"After your morning routine, you mean?"

"Of course."

She gave a genuine laugh. "Jimmie Mayfield, you never cease to amaze me. Keep your chin up. You'll hear soon enough, and I'm sure it will be positive."

"Thanks."

"Well, I should go. Tonight has not been a complete disaster, but I'm drained. And besides," she added, glancing behind them. "Clint's coming. I'm going to go."

She started to walk away as Clint got there. "Claire," he said with a casual nod.

"Clint. See you around, Jimmie." And she left.

Clint slid in next to him. "If you weren't a foot taller and a hundred and fifty pounds heavier than me, I'd be beating the shit out of you," said Jimmie.

Clint looked at his beer. "Told you, did she?"

"She did. Why did you do it?"

"Why not? They weren't together. Rob didn't try to get her back. And she's hot, so..."

"So, you betrayed your friend?"

"I didn't betray him. Rob could have gone after her. He didn't. He made his choice. I figured she was fair game. Especially since she wasn't coming back here. She was happy in Jacksonville, and it was a one-time thing."

"Wow. I can't believe you can rationalize it."

"Listen, the world's a shitty place filled with people doing shitty things. What's done is done. Telling him won't help things, will it?"

"No."

"Then drop it."

"I wish I didn't have to carry this secret."

Clint shrugged. "Shouldn't have talked to her then."

"Maybe you shouldn't have slept with her."

"Didn't we just go over this?"

"Are you at least sorry?"

Clint looked at him. "I learned a long time ago, regret is a wasted emotion. It changes nothing. I can't make amends for it, and telling Rob I'm sorry won't change it. Leave him blissfully ignorant, and everyone is happier. Besides, if Rob would not go after her, he needed to move on from her. She participated in it and is equally at fault. You give her the same grief?"

"No, I didn't. I thought there was a guy code."

"There is no guy code. People who say that are trying to stop you from doing something to them they've thought about doing to you. People down on snitches are doing shit that'll get snitched on." Clint finished his drink. "You want another? You probably need a drive too."

"Yes, please. To both."

"Myrna?"

They sat there with their beers. Clint took a gulp and turned to him. "Since we're here alone and being deep, what's the deal with you and Caroline?"

"Deal? There's no deal."

"Exactly. Yet for years, you've been holding a torch for her. She's not worth it."

"Why do you say that?"

"Listen, you are a traditionalist. You want to get married, have kids, the whole nine yards. You want a special woman. Part of you hopes it's Caroline."

"What, no...I...barely talk to her."

"And that's for the best. She's not the kind for you."

"Oh, you know the kind for me?"

"I know women," Clint said. "I do," he added as Jimmie arched his eyebrows. "Listen, you and she have several things in common. You both live with your mom, and neither of you has a job."

"What does it matter?"

"She's a user. Everyone in her life she uses. She came here by herself, didn't she?"

"Yeah, but..."

"How many girls you know go anywhere without a group of friends? None. She comes on her own because she has no friends. The girls she used to hang around with at school, most of them have settled down, are starting families. None of them want her around anymore."

"They are at different points in their life."

50

"It's because she's selfish and has nothing to offer. She was fun in school, but she's not someone they want around when things settle. Caroline's damaged and lonely. Almost makes you feel sad for her. I doubt she'll ever settle down."

"She's like you then."

"Not even close. I don't settle down because I don't want to get bored and hurt someone when I stray. And I would. So, if I start nothing real, I can't let anyone down, see?"

"Not really, but..."

"With her, it's because once people get to know her, the real her, they realize there's nothing they want there. Being pretty and having a nice set of tits will only get you so far. She'll give you nothing back. No love, no support, nothing. She's selfish. You've been thinking all this time she's out of your league. Forget that. She doesn't deserve you."

"What, like I'm such a catch?"

"Meh. That may be true, but you can do better than Caroline Ward. Hell, she's not even that good in bed. Women like that aren't. They give no part of themselves to you. She doesn't have to give any effort. Sure, she'll play you at first to catch your interest. You think you're getting a great catch, but you soon realize you got nothing. It's like sleeping with a sex doll; she'll just lie there and let you do your thing. She used to date a lot of guys back in school, right?"

"Yeah?"

"Do you remember her dating anyone for long?"

"No."

"You've got your answer about Caroline."

Jimmie didn't want to believe him. He'd harboured feelings for her a long time, but he lacked the confidence to make a move. He figured none of her relationships worked out because he and she were meant to be. Perhaps he'd been fantasizing about this for so long, he made himself believe it. But no matter how much sense Clint made, his feelings had

51

been set. It's hard to change your core beliefs, no matter how much evidence is provided.

"All right, so Mr. Love Guru, if she's not right for me, who is?"

"I don't have a specific person in mind, but you'd be better off with someone like Myrna."

"Myrna? You hate Myrna."

"Naw, she's all right. I antagonize her, yes, but as I said earlier, it's because she sees through me. She wants stability, holding out for the right guy. She's not giving it up for just anyone. The guy who gets her will find a strong, loyal woman who will give herself heart and soul to them. She's the anti-Caroline. Probably fucks like a tigress, too."

"It always comes back to that for you, doesn't it?"

"Yep," said Clint taking a sip. "I didn't say you should hook up with her. Someone like her."

"What, someone who won't sleep with you?"

"Bingo."

"You're incorrigible."

"Second time today, you told me that. You done?"

"Yeah."

"All right, let's go."

As they were getting up, he gave one last glance over at Caroline. She slow danced with a guy, a drink in her hand, throwing back her head and laughing at something inane and not witty the guy had said. She looked up at her dance partner, gave him a smile, bit her lip and started to kiss the guy on the neck. He looked like he just won the lottery. Unable to stand it any longer, he turned and followed Clint out the door.

Chapter 6

Jimmie slept in the next morning. He knew he slept in by the colour of Stacy Keibler's thong. Jimmie had been enamoured by her, and when he was sixteen, he bought her poster at the Port Charlotte Mall. Lovingly tacking it to the wall, she'd been his constant companion, watching over him as he slept. The poster also functioned as a sort of alarm clock; he approximated the time of day by the colours' intensity. If it was black or shades of grey, he needed to go back to bed. If her thong was bright blue, he'd slept in. His optimal wake-up time was when only a hint of blue appeared.

He lay in bed for a few moments, listening to the sounds of the park. "Man," he thought to himself, "yesterday was crazy."

He got out of bed and made his journey to the bathroom. Winked at himself in the mirror, conducted his business and back to his room to get dressed. Today, he felt like Batman, so he pulled out his Batman tank top. A pair of red lounge pants, complete with white lightning bolts, and he was ready to take on the world.

Frosted Flakes, Diet Coke, and a cigarette on the patio; the glamorous cocktail. And the sun on his face. He gave a sigh of contentment.

Today would be different. He could feel it. He got it, ok? The Fates had delivered their message to him. No more waiting. He could do something while he waited. Today he needed to get a job.

He'd need a resume. "It will be sparse," he said to himself. Can't put jobs he held for only a few days. "Going to be gaps."

Well, maybe he could say he helped his sick mother? She had lost her job, and he had been home with her, so it's not a lie, just embellished.

He'd go to the library to type it up and print. Do an internet search or read a book on resume writing, get ideas and suggestions on how he could design one to focus on his skills, not what he'd done. He liked it when a plan came together. Being focused on a plan kept the crushing despair at bay.

It had been years since he had a car. The old Corolla was long gone; Rob and he had taken a shortcut one day. It was back after high school, but before he had dated Claire, and there was this girl who interested Rob. She had a cousin visiting from Alabama who Rob thought would be great for Jimmie; they could double date.

"You know what girls from Alabama are like," said Rob.

"Yeah," he said, having no idea what girls from Alabama were like. He hoped it meant something good.

Their shortcut was an old dirt road. They had taken it before many times; it shaved off only five minutes on their drive, but when you're young and dumb, five minutes was an eternity. The human brain is not fully formed until you are twenty-five; he always thought this helped explain the myriad of idiotic things he and his friends used to do. But they could no longer use that excuse, and not much had changed.

The thing with their dirt road shortcut was, they only used it when it was dry. But Southwest Florida often gets heavy rain in September, and it was September. It had been raining the past couple of days heavily, even though the sun shone that day. They had been going along at a clip when they saw the puddle. "Hit it!" yelled Rob as he punched the roof of the car.

Jimmie gunned the engine and hit the puddle hard, water spraying high in the air. The further they went, the deeper it got, and the car came to a violent stop as the wheels sunk into the deep ruts of the tire tracks while the frame ground into the thick mud. This route had been well travelled in recent days by people in 4x4's; the Corolla didn't have the clearance of a 4x4, so it became stuck.

The two guys tried for forty-five minutes to free the car from the muck, but it was stuck fast. They were both covered in mud.

Jimmie and Rob walked along the dirt road and came across a farm field with an old farmer on his tractor. They explained their predicament and convinced him (for twenty dollars) to help tow the car out of the mud.

The farmer followed them to the trapped car. He unravelled the chain on the tractor and made them climb into the mud. "Attach it to the frame." He directed them from his dry perch on the tractor. "You attach it anywhere else, you're liable to damage the car."

Neither of them had the mechanical aptitude Clint had, nor could they see much in the muddy water. They attempted to loop the chain around what, in their estimation, was part of the frame.

"Ok, boys, if this goes wrong, don't blame me. You're the ones who put the chain on, remember?" The old man eased on the throttle, and the chain grew taut. His back wheels dug in, and the Corolla started to lurch out of the mud, a giant sucking sound making them aware of the mud's effort to keep in place.

It started to move. But they didn't check the depth of the water in front of the car. It was deeper than where it had rested. The front end of the vehicle sank lower and lower in the water.

"Stop!" he yelled, but it was too late. Straining against the grasping mud, the chain started to shudder, and the car, being constrained by the rear and being pulled hard in the opposite direction, gave a loud snap. The front axle gave way, and the tractor zoomed forward with the released tension. Slipping out of its original position, the car slid to rest in the deeper water. The entire hood of the vehicle submerged.

"You didn't attach it to the frame, now did ya? I warned you, boys." There was nothing more to do. The car was lost, stuck in the gripping mud. He'd have to replace the axle, which cost more than the car was worth. With the muck in the engine, he'd have to get it rebuilt. The car's ruined interior lay half-submerged in the muddy water. Jimmie abandoned it.

They unhooked the chain and gave it back to the farmer. Feeling sorry for them, the farmer gave the boys their twenty dollars back (although when things dried out, he came back, recovered the car and made a hundred dollars when he sold it for scrap). By the time they got out to the main road, and Rob got a cell signal (the back parts of Florida were sketchy on cell service), the girls had gotten pissed off and met up with two different guys. Rob's crush told him not to bother.

Jimmie had been without a car since then. He had a bike, but it got stolen. He had tried hitchhiking in the past, but he'd given it up after an incident. The driver that day was under the influence. Realizing his danger, Jimmie asked the driver to drop him off, and thanks for the ride.

"Sure thing. Hoss," the driver said. "Hey, you do drugs, man?"

Not a habitual drug user, he occasionally partook. "I'm not adverse. Why?"

"Got something here you might find groovy. A friend of mine in Tallahassee has been working on this little purple pill here," he said, holding up a pill bottle, "It will make you feel like Superman, you dig?"

"I dig," he said, feeling he was in a 1970s movie. Jimmie normally would not take drugs off a stranger in a car. But he rationalized, since he wouldn't be taking the drugs in the car with the guy, it was safe. He'd take it later and see what happened.

"All right, man. It's on the house. If you like it, there's an email on the bottle," the driver said. "You want more, drop them a note, and they'll set you up with as much as you need."

"Thanks."

That was his last memory. He didn't remember when he took the pill, but he woke up three days later in a lawn chair on a beach as the sun rose, wearing an American flag bandana, an American flag Speedo, a t-shirt with a screaming eagle holding an American flag in its talons, and one American flag flip flop. *This is a tad more patriotic than I am used to dressing,* he thought.

He limped his way home on his one flip flop to discover as he got undressed that he wore a woman's skimpy black thong and pasties over his nipples.

That was his last experience hitchhiking or using drugs stronger than alcohol.

Jimmie headed out of the park on his way to the library. The library was where he had spent many of his afternoons while working on the paralegal course. It was an hour walk in the unrelenting Florida sun.

He passed many strip malls along the way to the library. Forty minutes from home, he noticed a sign in the window of a local restaurant.

Help Wanted
No experience necessary
Apply within

He looked up at the overhead sign. "Flappers," it said. An all-day breakfast place. He'd had both good and bad experiences working in foodservice. His experience gave him a head's up over anyone else applying for the job. "Why not? What's the worst they could do? Hire me?"

The icy cold air conditioning of the place and the change from the heat outside made him shiver. The quiet of the restaurant unnerved him.

"Table for one?" asked the hostess as she came over to him. A short, older woman with a pleasant face, she smiled at him with a goofy look.

"No, thanks. I'm inquiring about the job."

"Really?" she asked, looking over the top of her glasses at him. "Ok," she laughed. She headed towards the kitchen. "Frank!" she yelled. "Some guy here about the job."

A man came out of the back. Overweight and sweating despite the air conditioning, his wrinkled white dress shirt fought to remain tucked into his pants. He had short brown hair and a sparse moustache. "You the guy about the job?"

"Yeah. What is it you are hiring? Busboy, dishwasher?"

The waitress laughed as she headed into the back. "No. It's in marketing," said Frank.

No experience needed in marketing?

"Yeah, this place is busy in the morning, and at 4:30, the seniors come in, but as you can see in the late morning, early afternoon, we're dead. I need someone to help us get customers in right now."

"Sounds good. What do I do?"

"This is under the table. I pay you cash at the end of every shift. You get to keep every penny. Five dollars an hour, for four hours a day, eleven until three. No breaks."

This sounded strange. "A hundred dollars a week?" It wasn't much, but it was better than being dirt poor. Add that on top of the small allowance his mom gave him, he should make do. It was one hundred more than he made now, and besides, he told himself, it was temporary. Once he got his results, he'd be on to bigger and better things. Even if he failed, he'd look for something permanent. "Sounds good to me. But what do I have to do?"

"You stand out by the road in costume and twirl a sign to get people's attention. Let them know we're here,"

Frank said. "I need you to dance and keep moving, you understand me? The last guy just stood around. That doesn't work. You need to be moving your arms, moving your feet. People need to notice you."

Jimmie wasn't keen on dancing outside in a costume for a hundred dollars a week. He almost rejected the job when he remembered what Rob had said, about thinking these jobs were beneath him. He needed humility. Besides, it wouldn't be hard. Stand outside in the sunshine, get a little exercise...and he reminded himself of its temporary nature. *It's not like this will be my career,* he told himself. *Just going to make some extra cash. Three weeks tops.*

"Ok," he said to Frank. "I think I can do that. When do I start?"

Frank looked at his watch. "It's almost 11 now. You can start right away. Come with me."

Jimmie followed Frank through the kitchen to a small utility area. "Here, put this on."

Frank handed him a giant heavy and faded foam flapjack costume. A circle revealed his face, his limbs jutted out between the pancakes, and a pat of butter rested on the front.

Looking at it with trepidation, he took the suit from Frank. The inside of the costume was damp from the sweat of the previous wearer. The high air conditioning prevented the suit from drying out. He eased his body gingerly into it, regretting the fact he wore a tank top with so much of his exposed skin coming into contact with the mouldering suit.

"Oh, this is gross." He could hear the waitress laughing somewhere.

"It fits. Here, take this sign," said Frank as he pressed a large white sign with red letters displaying the words 'All day breakfast: $3.99' into his hands. It was heavier than he expected. "You got to twirl it, but people need to read it too. It does no good if you are moving it too fast. Kind of make this motion." Frank appeared to be doing a weird hula dance, his belly jiggling beneath his shirt. "Nice and slow. And remember to keep turning around. You need to show the vehicles in both directions. Best if you do a count to yourself: one, two, three, four, five, six, seven, eight, and switch two, three, four, five, six, seven, eight, and switch. But don't count it too fast. Make them Mississippis."

"Yeah," he squeaked, still grossed out at the dampness pressing around him as the suit enveloped his body.

"We give you a bottle of water on the house. Here," Frank said, passing him water from the fridge as they passed. "You'll need it to stay hydrated. It's hot out there, and that thing doesn't breathe. You don't want heatstroke. Ration your water, move around, but not too fast, and you should be ok. Now drum up some business."

Frank held open the door for Jimmie, and the heat assaulted him in the suit. It was almost unbearable. "Where do I stand?"

"Right out by the road, near the parking lot entrance," said Frank.

"Not much shade out there."

"You need to be visible; otherwise, it doesn't work. Good luck, kid." He closed the door.

Jimmie hiked across the parking lot. He had to be careful as the suit blocked his peripheral vision. His legs didn't have full freedom of movement, and he couldn't put his arms down, making it awkward to move. It limited him to short, stuttering steps. He made it to his post and started his dance. "One Mississippi, two Mississippi..."

He grew hot. Not only did the sun beat on him, but the heat reflected off the asphalt. The fumes from the cars speeding by on the six-lane roadway made the air cloying. But even so, he danced.

He had not planned for lunch, and he grew hungry. He sipped at his water to stay hydrated and to stave off hunger. It disappeared fast. Better pace it. It had to last...he looked at his watch...another three hours and twenty-seven minutes. And what if he needed the bathroom? Frank had said no breaks. This couldn't mean...yeah, it did.

Rationing the water made it last longer, but looking at his watch, he saw he still had two hours and twelve minutes to go. The fact customers were entering the restaurant heartened him.

While Jimmie danced outside, unbeknownst to him, he was being watched.

"How's he doing?" Frank asked Carlo the busboy.

"I don't know, boss. He's slowing down. Starting to look woozy."

"Dumbass probably drank all his water already," said Frank. "At least he's got people to come in. But I don't want that little shit passing out. Not like the last guy did. Offer him another bottle. Tell him it's two dollars, and I'll deduct it off his pay."

Carlo grabbed a bottle from the fridge and took it to Jimmie. "Yo, flapjack. Frank says you look like you need water?"

He got light-headed and faint. His belly gnawed with hunger. "Yes, please."

"Boss says it's two dollars. He'll deduct it off your pay."

In his current state, he agreed. "Give it to me."

"Sure, dawg," said Carlo handing him the bottle. Jimmie took a swig. "Hey man, it's busier in there than I've seen in a long time. You're doing a great job."

"Thanks. Do you think Frank would let me eat? I'm starving."

"Nah, man. Frank won't want you dripping stuff on the suit."

"At least some toast? Maybe a Diet Coke?"

Carlo rubbed his chin. "I mean, I can ask him. He will charge you for it, though."

"I figured. Get me buttered toast and a Diet Coke, please."

"I'll see what I can do." Carlo headed back inside the restaurant. "Yo, Frank. Flapjack wants to know if he can get a Diet Coke and buttered toast?"

"What?" said Frank. "He can't dance and eat toast at the same time. Fine. You tell him because it's his first day, I'll make an exception. But tomorrow, he needs to plan this out better. Tell him it's four dollars for the toast and drink. I'm not making it until I know he's ok to pay for it."

Carlo opened the door and yelled at him. "Yo, Flapjack! Frank says it will be another four dollars. You ok with that?"

Thumbs up.

"We good boss."

Carlo brought him his order. "Thanks." Jimmie ate the toast. It helped take the edge off. The Diet Coke helped even better. The caffeine gave him the jolt he needed to get through the remaining...he looked again at his watch...fifty-seven minutes.

"Heads up, man. Watch out for the kids coming home from school. They can get nasty." Carlo headed back into the restaurant.

School kids. The bane of any mascot or costumed ad professional's existence. Doing the math in his head, he figured out the danger zone. His shift ended at 3:00. School gets off at 2:20, so he had sixteen minutes until school let out. Give them five minutes to get their school books together and head for home... the closest school he could think of was at least a fifteen-minute walk... the first kid might show up with twenty minutes left in his shift. That left a big window.

Jimmie fortified himself by downing the remnants of his drink. It energized him and readied him for whatever came his way.

He kept a solid pace. One Mississippi, two Mississippi...it was hard to keep an eye over his shoulder towards the school. Lucky for him, the wide-open and flat land meant they couldn't sneak up on him.

What he hadn't taken into consideration were bicycles.

Bicycles allow the kids to get there faster, and they allowed them to close the distance quicker. Jimmie didn't register on the bikes initially, looking for kids on foot. The squeals of delight first caught his attention. It threw off his rhythm as he spun around to face his tormentor. An eleven-year-old girl, her pigtails flying behind her, the big smile on her face revealing her braces, lead the pack of rascals. Her little legs pumped hard as she rose off her seat, her sundress flowing. Three boys and a girl descended on the pancake, grins on their faces, and mayhem in their eyes.

Everything slowed. The kids were getting closer by the second, but his legs were rooted to the spot. Then he started to turn away from them as a voice in his head said, "Run, Forrest. Run!" He began to run towards the restaurant.

He took four paces when he realized he would not make it.

The costume restricted his legs too much. He couldn't get a decent stride. And it's hard to run in Adidas flip flops under the best conditions. Besides, hunger and dehydration had left him weakened. The distance was too far, the kids too eager...

The girl tossed her knapsack, which got tangled in his feet, and he fell. Kids swarmed around him. They were throwing rocks. *Where did they get the rocks?* he thought. *Did they carry them around on the off chance they run into a pancake man?* He tried to use the sign as a shield to protect his face; the thick foam padding which had caused problems dancing in the sun protected his body from the assault, but his arms and legs were exposed. He tried to make his best turtle impression and pull his limbs into the protective shell.

An air horn cut through the roaring in his ears, bringing a respite from the attacks. "Hey, you little brats! Get out of here! You might damage the suit!" Frank hustled over as fast as his girth allowed. "Go on home, git!"

The kids rode away, laughing and giving each other high fives.

Frank came over and extended a hand. "You ok?"

"Yeah," He'd skinned his knee when he fell, and he had a few minor scratches on his arms and legs.

"Damn kids try that with every new guy. One guy who did this used to keep a slingshot on him to keep them away. Once you show your dominance by taking down one, they'll leave you alone. Pure rookie mistake, turning and running." Frank looked at his watch. "Almost done. Twenty minutes left."

"What? But I thought getting attacked ended my shift?"

"Why would you think that? C'mon get back out there. If you're lucky, you'll be done before the stragglers get here. If not, don't run."

For those last twenty minutes, he was a nervous wreck, assuming more kids would descend on him at any moment. Lucky for him, the remainder of his shift proved uneventful.

Entering the restaurant at the end of his shift, Carlo and the waitress greeted him with applause. Frank came over to him. "You won me ten dollars, kid. They bet me you wouldn't last until the end of the shift. I told them you had a whiff of desperation. The last few guys couldn't hack it. Here are your fourteen dollars." Frank handed him the crumpled bills. "I didn't even ask you your name when you got here. I don't bother until you've made it through one. What do they call you?"

"I'm Jimmie," he panted, peeling himself out of the disgusting suit.

"Happy to meet you, Jim. The lady is Denise, and he's Carlos." The waitress gave him a wave.

"Yeah, it's Jimmie. No one calls me Jim."

"All right, Jimmie, I'll remember that. You coming back tomorrow?"

Every fibre of his being screamed no. The words "yeah, sure" come out of his mouth uncontrollably.

"Excellent. See you tomorrow. Don't be late." Frank headed off into the bowels of the restaurant.

"Bye, Jimmie," said Denise.

"Dawg, the way you went down out there," smirked Carlo. "Much respect. See you."

64

Jimmie headed back into the heat. His hunger, abated by the toast, had returned. The day had left him too traumatized for Flappers, unable to look at a pancake. Casting his eyes around to see what was close.

McDonalds.

The McDonalds.

"Oh, no..."

He had no other choice. He was starving, and he needed to eat. Jimmie couldn't use the drive-through without a car. If he had a cell phone, he could order ahead on their app and limit his time in the restaurant. But he didn't have a cell phone. He had to go in. *It's okay*, he thought. *I doubt the pervert is even still working there. I'm sure they've found him out and fired him. Guys like that can't control themselves.*

Walking to the McDonalds, he looked in and noted the quiet. A few of the staff were standing near the counter, chatting, laughing. A single customer rang in their order at an automated kiosk. It seemed safe.

He strode through the doors, trying to exude confidence like he belonged there. He didn't feel it, but he hoped he projected it.

Using the automated kiosk was his best option. He frowned on this, preferring a person; McDonalds claimed nobody would lose their jobs because of the kiosks, but he didn't trust them. Why should he, knowing their hiring practices? Still, he felt it best to draw as little attention to himself as possible.

With the added cash in his pocket and his extreme hunger, he thought he would treat himself. He ordered three hamburgers, a small fries, a small strawberry milkshake and a large Diet Coke. Not having a credit card meant he had to pay at the counter. He wondered what the point was if he still had to interact with someone to pay as the machine spit out his order number: 342.

Jimmie went to the cashier. He handed over his payment when he heard the voice. The pervert was here.

The staff behind the counter were laughing with the assistant manager. *How could they?* he thought. *Don't they know he's a pervert?*

The pervert came around the corner. Jimmie shuddered at the gleaming skull the male pattern baldness displayed. He had on a pair of pervert glasses, those little round types with the thin wireframes, and his pervert moustache. His big belly pushed against the straining blue McDonalds' uniform shirt, spilling over the edge of his polyester pants. *Too bad it wasn't big enough to spill over and hide his offending member from sight.* Jimmie shuddered at the memory.

The pervert leered at him. *Maybe he won't recognize me?* he thought. *He'll remember me! No one else around here rocks this sweet mullet and chops combo. Damn me, and my vanity!*

"Order 342?" queried the woman behind the counter.

That broke him out of his fixation. "That's me," he said as he grabbed the bag of food and Diet Coke and headed for the door.

Behind him, he heard the pervert's voice. "Sir?" it said. "Sir? Wait a minute, sir."

Jimmie was not waiting a minute. He hurried to the door and opened it.

He could sense behind him the pervert on the move. "Sir, you forgot..."

"I forgot nothing! I remember it all!" Jimmie spun to face his tormentor.

The pervert stood there, a strawberry milkshake in his hand. "You forgot your milkshake," he said, holding it out, a confused look on his face.

"Oh," said Jimmie, reaching out to take it, careful not to make contact with his hand. "Thanks."

"Have a nice day," the pervert said as he smiled at him.

Jimmie turned and fled the restaurant, the staff behind him looking stunned.

Chapter 7

Friday night arrived. Rob had been persona non grata since Monday when he stormed out of the bar. He hadn't wanted to socialize, and true to Ryan's prediction, he had no interest going back to Gator's, at least in the short term.

Jimmie had been disappointed since he had pocket money for a change. If you prepared yourself for it, the job was palatable. He'd gone back the next day, wearing a t-shirt to limit the skin-to-costume contact, a pair of shorts and a pair of old New Balance sneakers. He had to be nimble. Oh, and lots of sunscreen; he hadn't realized until that evening how burnt he'd gotten.

Armed with two big old soda bottles filled with water and a light lunch (an apple, a bag of Zesty Cheese Doritos and ham sandwich, the healthiest lunch he had in a while), he was ready for anything. He got there early, stretched and climbed back into the horrid suit.

No longer starving and well hydrated, the day was better than his first. He even played with a few dance routines, mixing it up and keeping things interesting for himself. He got into a groove.

And at around 2:30 that afternoon, Jimmie readied himself for the inevitable.

He saw them coming this time. Wary and prepared, he put down his sign, picked up his surprise, keeping it out of sight behind his back, and strode out to meet them like a gunslinger of old.

The kids stopped thirty feet away, sensing the difference in their quarry. The leader stared right into his eyes, one foot resting on the ground, the other in anticipation on the high pedal. She slid her backpack off her back and held it in her left hand, her right hand gripping her handle grip. Every muscle taut, ready to spring into action, Jimmie raised himself up on the balls of his feet and waited.

Only the sound of the vehicles speeding passing them broke the silence. Staring each other down, like a bull and a matador, they waited for a cue to start the battle.

A slight tremor in the little girl's lip betrayed her. Her lip curled into a snarl, and she drove her foot down, rising in the saddle and twirling her backpack like a flail as she launched her bike forwards.

Time stood still. He willed his breathing to stop, clearing his mind of everything. The timing had to be right; she approached him quickly. The children waited for their signal to join the assault.

The backpack left her hand. Jimmie sidestepped the incoming projectile, feeling the air brush against him as it missed. Bringing his hand from behind his back, he brandished his secret weapon, an old broken umbrella, discarded at the side of the highway. He waited until the little girl passed by him to spring. Driving the umbrella into her front wheel spokes, the old umbrella's weakened metal held; it lodged there and jammed itself into the struts. The front-wheel became immobilized. Its forward momentum halted with the introduction of the foreign object, the bike pitched forward, and it launched the little girl over the handlebars of her bike to cartwheel to the ground. She landed on her back hard, knocking the wind out of her.

Time returned to normal. Jimmie threw up his hands in triumph. "Woo!" he shouted. He did a dance. "Woo!" He pumped his fist at the crying little girl. "WOOOOOOO!"

Looking at the kids, who were staring at him in disbelief, he yelled: "That's right! You want a piece of this? Huh?" The kids started to pedal away from him fast, tears streaming down their faces. "Go on, run away."

The little girl crawled to retrieve her backpack and got back onto her bike. "I'm telling my mom!" she cried as she started to ride away.

"Go ahead. You tell her you got your butt kicked by a pancake!"

At the end of his shift Frank, Denise, and Carlo looked at him, dumbfounded. "That was some fucked up shit," Carlo said. The kids never returned; as Frank had said, take one down and show your dominance, and they'll leave you alone.

"Great work this week, kid," said Frank Friday afternoon. "Business boomed on the afternoon shift. You're a natural. I'm giving you an extra ten dollars this week. Consider it your end of the week bonus. Every Friday shift you finish, you'll get an extra little something. See you Monday."

So yeah, he felt special that night.

Rob made it clear he wasn't going back to Gator's. "Hey, the bar they put in at Play Bowl! is nice. Maybe we should go there?"

"Not at my work," said Ryan.

"Why not? It's comfy there, they got a decent beer selection, and we might even squeeze in a game or two."

"Yeah. How about no? Why don't we go to the bar at Fairfield Marina? Got a great view of the boats."

"Hell, no. I'm not hanging out with those douchebags. Besides, I can't unwind there. It's my work. Someone I know might see me acting up."

"Exactly."

The three of them ended up at the saddest of bars: the strip mall Irish pub. A proper Irish pub needs character. Putting faux touches on a square box of space is a travesty. The clientele of the darkened pub was older than Gator's. The background din of the patrons drowned out the music. No chance they would run into anyone they knew.

"This ain't so bad," declared Rob. "This could end up being our place."

Ryan looked around with trepidation. "Well..."

"The first round is on me tonight, boys," said Jimmie.

"Whoa, what d'you do, rob a bank? Since when did you have the money to buy a round of beer?'

"Since I took your advice and got a job."

"You got a job?" asked Ryan.

"Tell me it's not giving blow jobs to retirees in the bushes at the golf course," said Rob.

"Classy. No, it's an actual job. At a restaurant."

"What are you doing there?" inquired Ryan.

"I'm helping them with marketing, you know, to drum up business."

"Marketing?" said Rob. "What do you know about marketing?"

"More than you. Shut up, or I'll rescind my offer."

They settled in and started to enjoy their beer.

"Listen, boys," said Rob. "I thought this Sunday we should check out the independent wrestling show going on over at St. Xavier's church hall."

"There's a wrestling show going on at a church this Sunday? On a Sunday?" said Ryan.

"It's in the hall, not the actual church, dumbass. And it doesn't start until four. It's only eight dollars. I think we should go."

"Count me out," said Ryan.

"What? No, you can't bail. We need you. You're our ride."

"Should have asked me earlier. I've picked up an extra shift on Sunday covering for Trudy."

"What, trying to get into some chick's good books by covering for her? While you're sitting at the alley, she will probably be out getting plowed by a real stud!"

"She's sixty-three. It's her granddaughter's christening."

"Oh. So how long is your shift?"

"I get off at four."

"Well, that should be plenty of time. So, we'll be late. I'm sure we'll still be able to get a good seat."

"Not sure, Rob, I..."

"I'll pay for your ticket."

"And my food?"

"What? No way."

"Have fun then. Maybe get Clint to take you."

"I asked. He said no. 'No interest in that local crap,' he said."

"Hey, why isn't he here with us now?" asked Jimmie.

"Said he was busy."

"Doing what?" asked Ryan.

"He didn't say. But I swear to Christ I saw his Jeep this afternoon parked at the marina."

"Oh, you don't think..."

"That's exactly what I think."

"Oh, shit."

"What are you talking about?" asked Ryan.

"We think Clint's 'offering his services' to a jerk at the marina. Or at least to the wife of a jerk," said Rob.

"Wow."

"Yep. Wow. The boy works fast," said Jimmie.

"The lure of the animal," agreed Rob. "Wouldn't believe it if I hadn't seen it myself."

"Back to your lack of a ride..."

"Come on, little brother. Oh, for Christ's sake, I'll buy you your food."

"And if I want a t-shirt?"

"Don't push your luck, bub."

"All right, I'll take you."

Jimmie had an idea. "Maybe Clint can drop us off at Play Bowl! early? We can grab a beer and watch the football game?"

"Bucs play the 1:00 game this weekend. Against the goddamn Saints. Fuck Drew Brees. I hate that guy."

"I guess if I'm not with you, the bar at Play Bowl! works fine," said Ryan. "And you'll be there when I get off."

"I got to take a piss," said Rob, downing the dregs of his beer. "Be right back."

Jimmie watched him go. "After you guys left, how was he?"

"It was dark. I let him rant and rave. He kept saying we should go look for hookers or something. Not getting a hooker with my brother. I wouldn't know where you'd look for one, to be honest. And it's icky."

"Yeah, but I doubt he was serious. He talks like that when he's down, but he'd never go through with it."

"No, he wouldn't. He ended up going home and drinking himself into a stupor. It made him late for work, so he got in shit. I think that snapped him out of it. But he's drinking harder than normal since then. He's frantic but better than he was." Ryan shrugged. "Give him time."

"Think he'll ask me about Claire? Does he know I talked to her?"

"I don't think he does. Did she say much? Did you talk to her long?"

"We did. And she did."

"What did she say?"

"If I'm going to tell anybody, it will be to Rob first," said Jimmie. "Sorry."

"I understand."

Rob came back. "Well, this place can't be our new spot."

"Why not?" said Ryan, relief displayed on his face.

"Hand dryers. It has those shitty old hand dryers in the John. The ones that wheeze on you like an eighty-year-old asthmatic. They just warm up your hands before you rub them on your shorts to dry." Rob had a real hang-up with hand dryers. His rants on them were legendary. "Either put in goddamn paper towels or upgrade to a hand dryer you stick your hands in. Let's get out of here."

They paid their bill and left.

#

Sunday came. Clint agreed to drive them to Play Bowl! "I should get my taxi license, the way I drive you two around," Clint remarked.

Dolores and Chester had stopped by the trailer so Dolores could pick up a few things. While she was in the bedroom, Chester leaned in close. "Did I see you dancing dressed as a pancake this week?"

"Yes, you did."

Chester shook his head. "Not what I had in mind, but I guess it's something."

The familiar ooga horn rang out. "I got to go."

"So," said Rob as they were speeding down the highway. "I thought I saw your Jeep at the marina on Friday."

"Your eyes still work," said Clint.

"So why were you there?"

"A gentleman never tells."

"Yeah, but you're not a gentleman. By anyone's definition of the word," said Jimmie.

"You're right. I'm not. I was injecting oxygen. And other things...boom!"

"We're to believe you met that rich woman on Monday, and by Friday, you're sleeping with her?" said Rob.

"More like by Wednesday. I told you both she was an inferno waiting to happen. She got a whiff of me, and she could not shake it. Man, she drained me so much this week my other ladies are suffering. I got nothing left to give!"

"Right. Sure."

"Do you doubt my sincerity?"

"I think you're full of shit. Jimmie, back me up."

"Yeah, back him up," said Clint looking at Jimmie in the rear-view mirror.

"Well..."

"You can't be serious? C'mon man, these stories are too much."

Jimmie might have agreed with Rob except, well, Claire. He thought Clint might be a sociopath.

"It's possible. It sounds incredulous but...I don't see why he'd lie about it."

"Boom!" said Clint.

"Wow, man. Seek help," said Rob, avoiding looking at Clint.

"She's a married woman, Clint," said Jimmie.

"So? That's between her and her husband. It has nothing to do with me. Maybe he shouldn't have left her alone." Clint gave a sideways glance at Rob.

It was uncomfortable being around them with this topic. Claire should never have told him. She unburdened herself but didn't need to put it on him. The bowling alley came into sight, so Jimmie could escape this situation.

"Hey, thanks, man, for the ride. Sure about not coming?" asked Rob.

"Nah. I'm a big-time guy. I'll leave amateur hour to the three of you."

They got out of the Jeep.

"See ya, fellas," Clint said. "Enjoy your sad afternoon of wrestling." He pulled out of the parking lot.

"I can't believe he moved in on Mrs. Monroe like that," said Jimmie as they watched Clint disappear.

"He's not even subtle. Not that he's ever subtle."

"You think he parked where he knew you'd see it?"

"He must have. That guy's getting worse, don't you think?"

"Yep. He's crossed a line."

"It will catch up with him."

#

The distinctive sounds of heavy balls rolling on a wooden floor and colliding with pins assaulted their ears as they walked through the sliding double doors into the bowling alley. Play Bowl! was baseball-themed; everywhere you looked, baseball dominated the decor. The bowling balls were painted to resemble baseballs, the pins like bats. Baseball photos and paraphernalia hung on the walls, and a colossal baseball mural spanned the back wall.

The (Extra)ordinary Life of Jimmie Mayfield

The entrance opened into an arcade half-filled with young families and people in their early 20s playing various games like Skee Ball and Deal or No Deal. Tickets spit out of the machines you could redeem for cheap prizes. When they headed to the lanes, they gave Ryan a nod. He was at the glass display case, a calculator in hand, helping a family with three screaming young kids to figure out if they would take the Army Parachute Man or a box of Rainbow Nerds with their last forty tickets.

Play Bowl! was quiet for a Sunday afternoon. Two lanes had families, a group of seniors at another. During the day shift mid-week, which Ryan worked, it was full of seniors playing in their league games. The audio tied into the electronic scoreboard further accentuated the garish baseball theme. If you got a strike, it flashed the words "Home Run!" on the screen, complete with roaring crowds; two gutter balls triggered a "You're OUT!" along with boos.

"Don't you find this place weird?" said Rob, looking around. "What's wrong with a simple bowling alley? Why make it look like a ballpark? It's not baseball."

"I guess the guy who owns the place likes baseball. Or the name stuck in his head, and he took it a few steps too far."

"Still weird," said Rob, shaking his head.

Given the theme, you'd expect it to carry over to the bar. Baseball might have worked there. Dark leather and metal predominated the bar, offering crisp, clean, modern lines. Jimmie imagined this is how the hotel bar in a fancy urban hotel would look, not that he'd ever been to one. It was out of place in the alley. Still, the bar had comfortable seats, big-screen TVs and a decent beer selection. Rob and Jimmie took up positions at the bar while a few mixed groups of seniors sat in booths enjoying their lunch.

Rob looked at his watch. "Kick off is in five minutes. Just in time." He nodded to the bartender. "What do you got for beers?"

"Draft or bottles?" she asked.

"Bottle. I'm a basic dude. Don't want nothing fancy."

"Since you're not fancy, can I offer you a Coors Banquet or a Coors Light?"

"Coors Light? I said I wanted a beer," he laughed out loud at his own cleverness. The bartender ignored it. "Do you have a Yuengling?"

"No, sorry, we don't."

"Bah, I'll take a Banquet then. What do you want?"

"I think I'll try a draft," said Jimmie, looking at the taps. "I'll take the IPA, please."

"Getting fancy now that you have a job. Soon you won't want to be seen with me."

"Well, I took a step outside my comfort zone this week, and it worked out ok. Thought maybe I should keep challenging myself and see what happens. Who knows, I might like it."

The bartender came back with their beer. "That'll be fourteen seventy-five."

"For two beers?" Rob said. "I could get four beers for that at Gator's."

"Sorry, but we're not Gator's."

Rob mumbled something to himself under his breath as he pulled out fifteen dollars. "Keep the change."

The game started. The sound was off. "I never understand bars that put a game on the TV but then have music playing," grumbled Rob. "It's even worse when it's a TV show or something you need to hear. Why bother?"

Jimmie took a sip of his beer and gave a shudder. "Ick."

Rob smiled at him. "What's wrong? Trying something new not working for you?"

"It's too hoppy. I don't like hoppy beer."

"Don't order an IPA then."

"I will get a Diet Coke."

Rob caught the bartender's eye again. "Can you turn on the sound? And my buddy wants a Diet Coke."

"Is Diet Pepsi ok?" she asked.

"I don't know," said Jimmie. "Is *Monopoly* money ok?"

"No," she said, annoyed at the two men sitting at her bar.

"Then no, Diet Pepsi is not ok. I'll stick with my beer, I guess."

The sound of the game replaced the music. "....the forty-ninth time these two teams have played, with New Orleans holding a thirty-one to eighteen lead in wins over the Bucs. They hold an eight and two record over the last ten games, with New Orleans knocking the Bucs out of the wild card hunt last December."

"The Bucs managed to hold Drew Brees to no touchdowns last year, which is almost unheard of in his stellar career..."

"Drew Brees," scoffed Rob. "I fucking hate that guy." He added loudly, "Go Bucs!" which drew several looks his way.

"I never understand this need for tribalism," said Jimmie.

"Tribalism? What the hell are you talking about?"

"This need to identify with a side. You see it in extreme patriotism, like 'my country is better than yours'."

"America is better than the rest! USA! USA!" hammered Rob.

"Have you ever been anywhere else?"

"Well, no."

"Have you ever compared how America stacks up against other nations on a variety of indices?"

"No."

"Well, then how do you know it's the best?"

"Because it is," stated Rob with absolute conviction.

"You're proving my point about tribalism. We want to identify with something. Where we are from, what religion we belong to, or don't belong to, to what sports we watch and teams we follow. We organize ourselves around these 'tribes' of people we identify with and proclaim our allegiance. Why couldn't you watch football because you enjoy the game? Why do you need to pick sides? You choose a side, they don't do well, and it makes you angry. It makes us direct anger at someone else who might wear a different team's logo on their shirt. You don't like the Saints because they beat the Bucs a lot?"

"Obviously."

"Would you hate them less if the records were reversed?"

"I might not hate them as much, I guess."

"You keep making my point."

"Point? The only points I heard were you slagging America and the Bucs to me. I got two points back for you." Rob flipped one middle finger up. "This one is for America." He flipped the other middle finger up. "And this one is for the Bucs. Two points, right back at you, buddy. Woo!"

The TV interrupted them. "Touchdown! And the Saints take an early six to zero lead over the Buccaneers."

"Sonofabitch! Fucking Drew Brees!"

"Guys, keep it down. Especially the profanity. You're disturbing the others," said the bartender.

"Sorry," said Rob. "Why do you say shit like this?"

"I have time to ponder; I read a variety of things. This is one I read about recently, and I wondered. I mean, I've followed no particular sports team."

"Because you hate sports."

"I don't hate sports, I don't understand the fixation, with the arguing that goes on between fans of different teams. It seems childish. I also am not religious, so I never understand why otherwise nice, decent people will be nasty to a group of people because they worship something different. Same thing with blind patriotism..."

"There you go slagging America again. You got a problem with freedom?"

"I don't see it as patriotic to ignore problems within our country because we are labouring under the belief we're the best, and we don't need to do better. We've been telling ourselves we're the best for so long, we believe it, without even bothering to check if it's true."

"You're lucky you're in this bar with these old people," said Rob, taking a sip of his beer. "They can't hear your blasphemy. And if they could, they're not likely to come over and punch you right in the mouth. Say shit like that in the wrong place, and it's liable to happen."

"I'm not saying America isn't awesome. I'm saying we shouldn't assume we're the best. We should work to make sure we are."

"You talk to Claire after I left on Monday?" Rob said, changing the subject.

Jimmie knew this would come. He looked at his beer. "What makes you think I talked to Claire?"

Rob shrugged, not taking his eyes off the TV. "You guys always got along well. You would talk when we went out as a group. If she were going to talk to anyone there, it'd be you."

"Yeah, we talked."

Rob nodded, still not looking at him. "My name come up?"

"How could it not."

"So, what did she say?"

"She's doing well up in Jacksonville. She was visiting her parents. Her dad's sick."

"He's not dying, is he?"

"I don't think so. She said he was under the weather. I doubt you'd say that about people who were dying."

"I'm happy to hear that. Jack was always good to me."

"Yeah."

"So, what did she say about me?"

"She knows she hurt you."

"That is an understatement."

"Claire said she still loved you."

"Funny way of showing it. You don't say no to a marriage proposal from someone you say you love. She tell you why she did it then? If she loves me so much?"

"Said she didn't want to be stuck in Englewood her entire life."

"What is wrong with Englewood?"

"You'd have to ask her."

"Pfft," went Rob, draining his beer. "That ain't going to happen."

"So, you don't want to talk to her?"

"Nope. That woman has done me wrong."

"Claire said she had hoped you'd come after her."

"She said that?" Rob finally looked at him.

"She did."

"Women. Always playing stupid games." They sat there, both staring up at the TV for a few minutes saying nothing.

"You think it's too late to go after her now?" asked Rob.

Jimmie didn't want his response to be the wrong one. "It might be," he said, trying to be noncommittal.

"Yeah."

They were distracted by the TV again. "Touchdown! The Saints take a thirteen-nothing lead with a minute thirty-two left in the second quarter."

"FUCK!" said Rob, too loudly. "Goddamnit!" This elicited a look from the bartender. "Sorry," he told her. "Don't worry, we're going. Drink your hop juice, and let's go. I can't watch anymore, and besides, this place is too lame to watch a game in, not to mention the cost of the beer."

"Nah, I'm done. It was all right, just not for me. What the hell should we do?"

"I don't know. Want to bowl?"

"No. I'm not interested in wearing communal shoes."

"The arcade?"

"I'd rather not spend my limited funds on amusing games of chance to win tickets I can redeem for junk I don't want."

"You're killing me, dude. Seriously."

Lucky for them, as they walked out of the bar and into the lanes, they ran into Ryan.

"Place is dead. They said I could go early," said Ryan.

"Great, because your bar sucks, and Jimmie is depressing me. Let's go. I want to get a great seat."

#

They went out into the parking lot and got into Ryan's Toyota Matrix. "Still bugs me you didn't buy American," said Rob.

"I used to own a Toyota," said Jimmie.

"That was different. You bought that used. This guy bought his brand new. You got what was decent and available and could afford. This guy could choose anything, and he chose a Japanese car."

"You don't have to drive in it, you know," said Ryan

"Whatever. Just drive."

"Who's headlining the matches today," asked Jimmie.

"The Lucas Boys are defending their tag team belts against Handsome Jack and The Great Pandolfo. Ladies on the card too. Gloria Gains against Suzy Foxx. Bunch of others I've never heard of." Rob turned around in his seat. "You want to see people you recognize, come up to Sarasota to the WWE show."

"Nope. Pass. Not going to Douchebag City."

Rob turned front again and shook his head.

They pulled into the virtually empty parking lot at St. Xavier's. The sign out front declared 'This Sunday, Florida XXXtreme Wrestling show. Tickets eight dollars'.

"Doesn't triple X's imply adult entertainment?" asked Jimmie.

Rob shrugged. "No sexy stuff going on in a church hall."

"Then why call it that?"

Rob threw up his hands. "Why do you question everything? Why can't you just enjoy it and shut up? Always 'why this' and 'why that'. Christ."

"So sorry. I'd rather not go through life ignorant of everything."

Ryan slid the car into a spot. Rob leapt out, annoyed by the whole line of discussion. "Looks like we got here early

81

enough to get good seats, boys. One thing going for me today."

A tired-looking woman in her fifties with thick owl-like glasses and an unnatural orange tint to her hair sat inside the door. Her neckline plunged low, exposing overly tanned, wrinkled skin. "Eight dollars each, fellas," she said with a rough, raspy, disinterested voice.

Rob handed over a twenty-dollar bill. "For him, and for me," pointing at Ryan.

She peeled off four singles. "Eight dollars sugar."

Jimmie handed over his money. "Do we have assigned seats?"

The woman laughed. "Take whatever seats you want. Take two of them. I don't care."

They went into the auditorium. On one side of the space were extended collapsible bleachers. On the other side were thirty chairs.

"Doesn't look like they are expecting much of a crowd," remarked Ryan.

"I'm sure it will be packed soon enough," said Rob.

The hall was far from packed. An obese guy wore an old faded and stained purple 'Macho Man' t-shirt and track pants, his awkward-looking girlfriend sitting next to him. A guy in his sixties with bottle-blond locks, a leather biker jacket and a pair of zebra-patterned Zubaz pants paced along the top row of the bleachers. A father in a trucker cap and leather vest sat with his two kids, both of them playing on cell phones, disinterested in where they were.

"Remember, you need to buy me snacks," said Ryan to Rob. "I'm feeling extra hungry. Going to get a large popcorn, a hot dog and a Twix bar."

"Jesus. Fine. Jimmie, grab us three seats, will yah?"

"Ok. Floor or bleachers?"

"Floor seats give us backs to our seats. But the bleachers give us a better view of the ring because we're up higher. Your call, I guess."

Rob and Ryan left. Jimmie scanned the venue, trying to decide. He took the middle of the second-highest row of the bleachers, figuring they gave the best view. While he waited for the brothers to get back, he noticed more patrons starting to drift in.

The guys came back. "Why did you pick so high?" said Rob as he sat.

"You said it was my call. Speak up next time if the height is an issue."

"We're so far away from the action. It'll do. I guess."

Ryan spread out his food on the bench beside him. "This guy will eat me into the poor house. The hot dog alone was seven bucks," said Rob.

"Maybe think of that before you drive through the front doors of a liquor store."

Rob scowled at him but said nothing. He looked at the entrance. "Oh, look at these guys coming in."

A group of developmentally challenged men entered, escorted by volunteers. "Hey, look. Myrna's with them."

"Myrna?" said Rob. "What's she hanging out with those retards?"

"Come on, Rob. Don't use that word."

Rob rolled his eyes. "Sorry. You're right, I know. Just don't make a federal case about it."

"I make it a 'federal case' because I know you're better than that. You need to be reminded periodically."

Rob looked at his feet and sighed. "Sorry." His sorry this time was genuine.

"Soowd wi sy hi?" asked Ryan, his mouth full of popcorn.

"Yeah, I will. I'll see if she wants to come to sit with us." Jimmie climbed down the bleachers and went over to where she sat. "Hi, Myrna."

She turned to him, her big smile fading. "Oh, hi."

"Hi."

"You said that."

He blushed. "Yeah, I guess I did. I'm here with Rob and Ryan," he said, turning and pointing over his shoulder to where they were. Ryan gave her a wave. "I thought I'd come and see if you wanted to sit with us."

"Well, that's sweet," she said as she waved back at Ryan. "I'm sitting with Harry," indicating the guy beside her. "Harry, say hello to my friend Jimmie."

"Hello," said Harry with a big smile. "We're here to watch wrestling."

"Hi, Harry. Yeah, my friends and I are here to watch wrestling too."

"Ok," said Harry. "Bye, bye."

Myrna smiled and shook her head. "I volunteer at the St. Alban's group home. These guys are residents there."

"We took a bus," said another man.

"This is Earl. Earl, meet Jimmie."

"Is Jimmie your boyfriend?"

Myrna blushed. "No, Earl, he isn't."

"That's good," said Earl, giving Jimmie a hard look.

He remained there, awkwardly. Myrna needed to help the men she chaperoned. "You guys have fun. I'll see you around, Myrna."

"Speaking of which, I didn't see you guys at Gator's since Monday."

"Yeah. Rob didn't want to go back after the Claire incident. I don't know when we'll be back."

Myrna gave him a slight smile. "You can come without him, you know. You don't have to do everything he wants to do."

"I guess I can. I have been trying things outside of my comfort zone as of late."

Myrna laughed. "All right. See you."

"You too, Myrna. Bye, Earl, Harry. Enjoy the show." He walked back to his seat.

"What's she doing with those guys?" asked Rob. "She didn't want to sit with us?"

"She volunteers at their home."

"The things you'd never guess about people, huh?" said Ryan.

"Yeah," said Jimmie.

Ryan looked at his phone. "Hey, Rob, Bucs scored three unanswered touchdowns in the fourth quarter. Kicked

84

the game-winning field goal with ten seconds left on the clock. They won thirty-four to thirty-two."

"Ah, shit."

"Hey, they won. That's something."

"Yeah, but I missed it. I've been missing out on lots of things lately."

The show got underway. The wrestling was uninspired, but the St. Alban's residents, sitting along the front of the bleachers three rows ahead of them, were enjoying it. Jimmie could not help but glance at Myrna during the show, watching her laugh and joke with Earl and Harry and the others. *The things you'd never guess.*

Troy Young

Chapter 8

The sun had gone down an hour ago. The world outside the trailer was quiet; only the McCarthy's muted argument penetrated the thin metal walls like the buzzing of an insect. He and Dolores sat at their kitchen table, its Formica top looking yellow in the dim light cast by the single 60-watt bulb illuminating the inside of the trailer. A large envelope rested on the table.

Jimmie sat there staring at the envelope, both hands resting beside it. Dolores shifted nervously in her seat, glancing from the envelope to his impassive face and back again. "Jimmie..."

"Six to eight weeks, my ass. It's been nine and a half," he said. Still, he sat there, staring at it.

It had been an uneventful three and a half weeks for Jimmie. He had settled into his job at Flapper's; not only had he developed a whole series of dance routines, but with four hours a day, five days a week in the hot sun wearing a thick foam suit while being in constant motion, Jimmie found himself in the best shape of his adult life. He'd always been on the skinnier side, but his lack of exercise and a terrible diet had left him soft and with low levels of energy. The intense exercise and his better, packed lunches had made him lean and feeling energetic, better than he had in years. He'd saved one hundred and thirty-seven dollars above his weekly needs.

Business at Flappers had been brisker than ever, according to Frank. People commented on how the dancing pancake made them check the place out. Jimmie developed a few fans; regular travellers began honking and waving at him as they drove. Sometimes, he'd even get a "Woo! Pancake man! Woo!" His friends discovered where he worked. They had a laugh at his expense, but then they bought him a beer and congratulated him for having the guts to go out and at least do something.

Rob allowed himself to return to Gator's. After a few visits, he stopped looking around every time the door opened, half expecting Claire to enter. He never brought her up, and Rob's attitude had shifted from a burning distaste towards her to a sense of melancholy. Jimmie speculated that Rob hoped to see her enter.

Clint, against the odds and history, was still seeing Luther Monroe's wife. He even started talking about her to his friends, referring to things Nancy had done or things Nancy had said. His comments were less graphic and less misogynistic than usual. They were both relieved and distressed by this revelation.

Ryan's life remained unchanged. Nothing ever changed in Ryan's life. Good old boring, dependable Ryan.

Chester and Jimmie interacted a few times; Jimmie had learned about the world of commercial fishing, and Chester had not once used a derogatory term like retard. Chester had even bought him an old bike. "It's nothing special," said Chester, "but it works. It'll make it easier to get to your job." Chester gave him a big smile. He had to hand it to Chester; he made an effort.

And then the envelope came.

"Are you going to open it, dear?"

"I am. It's been so long I've waited for this; now that it's here, I'm in a state of shock. I need to prepare myself."

"You think it's good news?"

Jimmie pondered for a moment. It was a large envelope, not a regular-sized one. "Well," he began, "I assume if it were bad news, they would have sent me a simple one-page letter in a standard #10. And," he picked it up and held it in his hands, fanning it, "there is a thin sheet of cardboard in it like they use to protect something important. Such as a certificate."

Dolores took out a joint and lit it. She took a big drag to calm her nerves. She shook in anticipation. "Oh, for fuck's sake, open the goddamn thing! You're killing me!"

"Mother! You normally don't use such language."

"We've been sitting here for two hours!"

"Ok." He took a deep breath, picked up the envelope, and tore it open with his fingers. He slid out the contents and laid them flat.

"Dear Mr. Mayfield," he began, a quiver in his voice. "We are happy to inform you that you have passed the Certified Paralegal (CP) exam. This qualifies you to further your studies and sit for the Florida Certified Paralegal (FCP) exam. You are eligible to apply for admission to the Paralegal Association of Florida (PAF) or your regional paralegal association...."

Dolores gave a squeal and came around the table, giving him a solid hug and kissing him on the top of his head. "I'm so proud of you," she said, tears welling up in her eyes. "I knew you'd do it!"

"Mom, please. There's still more." He shuffled through and pulled out another piece of paper, this one with the letterhead of the Monroe Group on it. "Congratulations," he read. "As a recipient of a Monroe Group Educational Grant, and for having achieved a qualifying final grade on your CP exam, you are granted an interview at the Monroe Group for the role of Junior Paralegal. As the State of Florida's third-largest law firm and seventh largest in the southern United States, we have a growing need for qualified individuals such as yourself. Please contact us at your convenience to set up your interview." Jimmie stared at this letter in disbelief. It was signed by John Demetos, Junior Partner, The Monroe Group, Port Charlotte Office.

"I'm going to have an interview." He continued to stare at the letter, reading it over two times to make sure it said what he thought it meant. "They want to interview me! He called me a 'qualified individual.' I'm a qualified individual!" He continued to look through the pile and alighted on his certificate. There was his name 'Jimmie Mayfield' in calligraphy on the page. It said he had passed the Certified Paralegal (CP) exam. Two words jumped off the page for him: "With Distinction," he said in awe.

Jimmie found the transcript of his final mark. He sat there, stunned, looking at it.

"What is it?"

"My mark. I got a ninety-eight. A ninety-eight. I've got nothing approximating a ninety-eight in my life."

Dolores gave another happy squeal, clapping her hands together as she stomped her feet and spun herself in a circle, shaking her head from side to side. "Oh, I always knew you were smart. When you commit yourself, you can do anything. Anything!" She grabbed his face in both hands, squeezing his cheeks together and covered his face with sloppy kisses.

They heard a tentative knock. "Can I come in?" asked Chester. "I've been sitting on the patio for two hours, and it sounds like there's a party."

Dolores looked at Jimmie, asking him permission for Chester to come in. Jimmie gave her a nod. "Come in here, you big beautiful man!"

The door opened, and Chester peered around the corner of it. "Sure sounds like good news."

"Oh Chester, he not only passed, but a big firm wants him to come in for an interview! He will be working in a fancy law office!"

"Well, that's great news! Way to go, my man! You never cease to surprise me. When your mother told me you were working on this thing in secret and finding out today how it went, I didn't know what to think. But this is great. Just great."

Dolores went over to Chester and wrapped her arms around him. "He passed his exam, and now my two men are getting along so well. This is such a great day." She turned to

Jimmie. "You've got a lot to do to get ready. Call that man first thing tomorrow. You will have to go get proper clothes for your interview; you can't show up at that office in a tank top and lounge pants."

"Maybe get a haircut, too," said Chester.

The Mayfields both looked at him. "Why? He's so handsome the way he is."

Chester knew better than to challenge her on that one. "Right. I meant a trim. Nothing makes a man feel like a million bucks than a nice trim. That's all."

"You'll need a few white dress shirts, a few pairs of nice khaki pants, a dress belt, nice shoes and a tie or two. Chester, can you drive us to Walmart this weekend?"

"Mom," said Jimmie rolling his eyes. "I'm going for an interview with the third-largest law firm in Florida. I can't get my work clothes at Walmart. Chester, can you take us to Target?"

Troy Young

Chapter 9

The interview was at hand. He'd called Mr. Demetos the next day and set up an interview for the following Monday morning at 9:30 am. This gave him the weekend to go to Target and let his friends know what he had done. He had to tell Frank he might be late for his shift at Flappers on Monday.

"Late?" exclaimed Frank. "I don't abide by late. We have a very set day. You work eleven to three, no exceptions."

"Well, I'm sorry. You must make an exception. I have an appointment."

"What kind of appointment does someone like you have?"

"I've developed this weird mole. The doctor thinks it might be skin cancer. Asked me if I'd been spending time out in the sun lately. I told him no. For now." Frank blanched. "It's probably nothing. My appointment is at 9:30. I might not be late. I wanted to tell you in advance."

"I guess it doesn't get busy until at least noon. And Monday is our slowest day. But, if you don't start wearing your sunscreen as I said you had to do if you wanted to work here, I might have to fire you."

"I'll try to remember. Sometimes I forget to bring it with me." The next day, when he showed up for work, a big bottle of sunscreen sat on the shelf near the flapjack costume. Frank worried he'd be fined for a workplace violation. Even though he got paid under the table, enough people had seen the pancake man. It would be tough to prove he didn't work here if it came to that, which had implications of tax violations. The government will sometimes look the other way, but not when it comes to money they were owed and didn't receive. Frank didn't want the IRS on his ass.

When he told his friends he had been studying in secret and now had a job interview for a professional job, it took them by surprise. "Wow, I always knew you were the smartest of us," said Rob. "I almost feel bad giving you grief about being a lazy dipshit. Almost."

"Congrats Jimmie," added Ryan.

"Shit son, that deserves a beer. Hey Myrna," shouted Clint. "Bring my boy here a beer, on me. He's going big time on us."

Myrna brought him his beer. "What does he mean?"

"I have a job interview to be a paralegal at the Monroe Group."

"That the firm with the billboards and TV ads?" asked Myrna. He smiled and nodded, hardly able to contain his excitement. "Wow, that is something. Don't you need to go to school to become a paralegal?"

"I did it by correspondence over the internet. Spent days at the library working on it. I ended up with a ninety-eight."

"Myrna, you better get out of the blast zone. That swelled head of his is liable to blow at any time," laughed Rob. "Then, you'll be covered with brains and bodily fluids." Clint snickered, while Ryan shot his brother a sideways glance.

Myrna ignored Rob. "That's fantastic. I always knew there was more to you than you'd expect. When's the interview?"

"Monday morning. I can barely wait."

"You'll do great," said Myrna smiling at him. She touched him on his arm and went back behind the bar.

"Boys, our boy here might soon get to be too big-time to hang out with us. Going to be hanging out with his new douchebag legal friends, you watch. Might even take him up to Sarasota!" laughed Rob. "He'll be at the marina, partying it up on the bosses' boat. Speaking of which," he said, turning to Clint. "Haven't seen your Jeep around lately. You and her Ladyship done exploring each other?"

"Nope," said Clint, taking a swig of his beer. "I couldn't keep showing up there. People might see me. Those boats are close together; she's a real screamer. She's been coming over to my place daily. People are used to hearing women scream in ecstasy at my crib."

"Daily?" said Jimmie.

Clint nodded at him. "Doesn't this go against your normal method of operations?" asked Ryan.

"It does. She's quite the woman. Not only is she a filthy beast in bed, but I talk to her. I don't talk to the women I carry on with because they got nothing interesting to say. Besides," he said, looking at his beer but not focusing on it. "She's married, and we have no expectations. We are riding this wave while it lasts."

Clint wasn't convincing. This woman had gotten to him

On Saturday, Chester drove the Mayfields to Target. Jimmie had his savings with him, and Dolores had a few bucks to kick in too. Either she had an extra little set-aside Jimmie hadn't known of, or Chester had given her money to help. He bought three white dress shirts, three pairs of dress khakis (black, navy blue and beige), a black dress belt, black dress shoes and two ties (a red and a blue). He'd had his eye on this great tie; it had a cat on it, its claws raised with lightning bolts shooting out of its eyes up into a starry sky. It was a sweet tie, but maybe it was too much for his first week. He swore to himself he'd come back and buy it once he got his paycheque; it was a second month at work thing.

The weekend was over before he knew it. Jimmie was so excited about his new stage in life. He was sure he'd get the job.

Jimmie studied how to write a resume and had forwarded something he had written to the Monroe Group. He decided since he didn't have relevant work experience to put on it, he'd put nothing. Instead, he highlighted his education, the skills he'd learned, pointed out his impressive final score and gave personal information he thought might be relevant. He already secured the interview, so he supposed it didn't matter.

Stacy Keibler was staring down on him somewhere in the dark, the excitement making it unable to remain asleep. A quick stop in the bathroom and then onto the kitchen. His Diet Coke and Frosted Flakes mingled with his cigarette out on the patio. He had no time to linger today.

Jimmie needed to get into the proper headspace as he got ready. This was a big day. He needed to be perfect. The occasion called for just the right music. Digging out an old cassette, he pressed play, and the heavy opening of Survivor's 'Eye of the Tiger' erupted from the speakers of his old boom box.

He brushed his teeth twice (he even flossed) and took out a small pair of trimming scissors, cutting any errant nose hairs and wiry eyebrows. Using a small comb and combing his mutton chops, he trimmed any whiskers which struggled to lie flat. A glance at his hair. "Perfect," he said—no need to touch it.

He went into his room and put on his shirt and his black pants. Opting for the blue tie as Luther Monroe always wore a blue tie in his ads. He then realized Luther always wore a navy suit, so he changed into his navy pants.

Chester had agreed to drive him this morning. "You can't take your bike to your interview," said Chester. "You'll be sweaty and your hair out of place. I'll take you."

Jimmie walked through the trailer, took a swig of soda out of the bottle in the fridge to help calm his nerves, and headed out to the patio.

It shocked him to see his friends there, along with Chester and his mother. They had stretched a big sign between the palm trees that read, "Go get him, Tiger!" His friends hooted and hollered and clapped their hands when he came out.

"Shouldn't you guys be getting ready for work?" Jimmie blushed.

"We told them we'd be late today," said Ryan.

"Yeah, your first shot at a real job since...well forever," said Rob. "This is a historic day." With his hand over his heart and a solemn look at Clint, he said: "Mark this down." Clint patted himself, miming looking for a pen and a pad of paper. "On this day, our little Jimmie Mayfield becomes a man."

"Didn't Gloria Clifford do that out behind the school senior year?" asked Clint.

Rob laughed. "Yeah. It's what turned her into a lesbian!"

"Guys, c'mon. This is already stressful for Jimmie," said Ryan.

"Oh, you boys," added Dolores. "You are such jokesters. I know my boy is saving himself for that special someone."

"Mom!" said Jimmie, exasperated as his friends roared with laughter.

"All right," interrupted Chester. "We best be getting a move on. You don't want to be late for the interview."

"Let's go." His friends yelled different variations of "Good luck" and hooted at him as he got into Chester's blue Chevy Impala. "Thanks," he said to Chester when they were in the relative quiet of the vehicle.

"It's good to have friends who support you," said Chester. "But there's something off with those guys. Well, except the quiet one, he's ok."

"They're ok. They mean well. I put up with the teasing."

They drove to the Monroe Group's office in relative quiet. Chester had jazz playing on the radio. The office had its own building along a busy highway strip, with a CVS on one side and a Bob Evans on the other, a shiny two-storey glass and white stucco building emblazoned with the blue and gold Monroe Group sign. A billboard with Luther Monroe sat on the top of the building.

"Good luck. I can wait around for you. I'll sit in the Bob Evans and get a coffee, read the paper. Your mother would appreciate that."

"Thanks, Chester. I don't know how I'd get home or how I'd call you to get me."

"All right then, you get in there. Show them that 'Eye of the Tiger'."

Jimmie strode to the door, brimming with confidence. Electric double glass doors slid open as he approached, and a wall of air-conditioned air and a busy cacophony of sound hit him as he entered.

The place bustled with activity. The half-full waiting room held a variety of characters. Behind the reception desk sat a pleasant woman with a round face. He could see cubicles and a glass door over her shoulder, which led back to more offices.

"Hello there," she greeted him as he walked over to her. "How may I help you?"

"I have an interview this morning with John Demetos and Gina Plummer."

"Well, isn't that nice. Who should I say is here?"

"Jimmie Mayfield. They are expecting me."

"I'll let them know you are here. Please have a seat."

A diverse crowd scattered throughout the waiting room. A gentleman with a pair of crutches and a neck brace and two black eyes sat in a chair. Over further was a tiny old woman with thick coke-bottle glasses clutching a paper bag filled to bursting with old documents. An overweight woman with frizzy hair and too tight a t-shirt sat on her phone, intermittently looking up to yell at her two young boys who caused a nuisance.

Jimmie watched the people for a while, intent on observing those he might be soon helping. His eyes wandered up to the large screen TV suspended from the ceiling. One of the 24-hour cable news networks was on with the sound off and the closed captioning on. He read the scroll across the bottom of the screen: *Senate passed the 34th Amendment to the Constitution. Heading to the states for ratification...Amendment lowers the age to run for President to 30 from 35...Rumours have President proposing Amendment to Republican Leaders as he hopes to replace Vice-President on the ticket for the next election with his daughter...*

The double doors slid open, and there stood Luther Monroe. Resplendent in his navy suit and blue tie, the diamond in his pinky ring causing the light to dance, his hair held in place with a thin sheen of gel, and his sparkling eyes and cheerful round face scanning the room.

"Good morning Kathy," he said to the receptionist, his silky voice recognizable from his TV and radio ads.

"Good morning, Mr. Monroe," said Kathy.

Luther approached the individuals in the waiting room. "Thank you for choosing the Monroe Group to help you in your troubling times," he said, a calming and dulcet tone disarming everyone. He took everyone's hand in both of his, in a comforting grasp, looking them right in the eye and giving a warm nod before moving on to the next person. "We know you could take your case anywhere, but you've come here. To us. To our family. And we will do our best to get you the settlements you deserve. My grandfather started this firm to help the people of Florida, and we continue with his vision today. We're here," he paused for dramatic effect as he reached out for Jimmie's hand, looking him right in the eye. "We're here," he repeated, "Fighting for you."

Jimmie let out an involuntary squeal, barely audible. He realized he had been holding his breath since the moment Luther walked into the room. Somewhere, in the deep recesses of his being, he found the ability to speak. "Thank you, Mr. Monroe; it's a great honour and a privilege to be here, sir. I don't have a case. I'm here for a job interview. I want to fight for these people."

Luther gave him a quizzical look. "Oh, you're here for an interview, are you? Did you drop a resume off with Kathy then?"

"No, sir. I have an interview set up with Mr. Demetos and Ms. Plummer."

"Ah," said Luther. "That's great to hear, son. Listen, if John likes you, I know we'll like you. He's a shrewd judge of character. Sorry, I don't think I caught your name, son?"

"Jimmie. Jimmie Mayfield, sir."

"Well, Jimmie, good luck to you. Perhaps I'll be seeing you around then."

"I hope so, sir. It's my dream to work here at the Monroe Group."

Luther nodded and turned away. He walked past Kathy's desk and through the glass door into the back.

#

Jimmie floated as he walked across the parking lot to the Bob Evans where Chester waited for him. "How did it go?"

"It went great! I aced their questions, and my passion impressed them. I know they will offer it to me!"

"That's awesome. Your mom will be so proud."

The smiles would not stop.

100

Chapter 10

Jimmie was ecstatic when John called him with the news; he'd gotten the job. They scheduled him to start the next Monday. He needed to let Frank at Flappers know he was leaving.

It floored Frank. "Listen, kid, you are the best. The best. I've never seen a mascot like you. Business has never been better. Listen, I'll double your salary. $10 an hour. What do you say?"

"I'm starting a job paying me $37,000 a year to start, with full benefits and a 401k. It's my dream job; I don't think you can compete. And if you can double my salary now, why didn't you pay me that once you knew how good I was?"

"You will ruin me, you know," said Frank, ignoring the inquiry. "No one lasted more than a week and a half. You're a natural. You don't know what you are doing."

"I think I do."

"Bah," said Frank. "When it goes to hell for you, don't come crawling back here, you hear? You walk out that door, it's done. I can't believe you're leaving. You're ungrateful. After what I've done for you. Fine." He started to walk away but turned back to ask: "You will stay until Friday, at least, right?"

"Of course."

"Good, good." Frank walked away without a glance back.

Jimmie spent an anxious weekend at the trailer, going over his study notes, trying to remember everything he had learned (ten weeks was a long time not to access the information you had been learning).

He couldn't see Stacy Keibler in the darkness when he woke. There was no time to linger on the patio with his Frosted Flakes, Diet Coke and a cigarette. Jimmie gulped his cereal, washed it down with a swig of soda, and had his cigarette on the bike ride to his office. He let his mind linger on that...his office...it gave him tingles.

It took him forty-two minutes to bike to the office. He tried to go nice and slow so as not to show up sweaty. That early in the morning, it helped it was still cool out. He glanced at his watch; he was twenty minutes early. He went to Bob Evans and had toast and jam. If you are going outside your comfort zone, you might as well go way outside of it; he almost ordered a coffee but figured there was a limit to leaving your zone.

He walked through the sliding doors of the office and surveyed his domain. There were no clients in yet; the calm of the office soothed him as he entered. Kathy smiled at him as he approached. "You're back. Glad to see you again. It's wonderful you will be joining us. Follow me, and let's go tell Rebecca you are here. She's in charge of the paralegals."

Jimmie followed her into the back. Rebecca had bright red hair teased out in a style contemporary to his own and wore a thick cardigan and a pashmina against the air conditioning. "Hi, you must be Jimmie," she said with a smile, getting up and extending a pudgy ring-encrusted hand to him. "I will show you around the office and point out where things are and then," her smile faded. "I'll introduce you to Gil Lemon. You will work only with him."

"Is it normal to be assigned to one lawyer?"

"No," said Rebecca hesitantly. "Gil's...special. He doesn't...doesn't work well with others. Luther must have seen something special in you to hire you to work with Gil."

"Thanks, Rebecca. I will leave you here." Kathy retreated to the front.

The tour of the office took half an hour. Jimmie learned where they stored the files, where the copiers and fax machines were, and found his work station. They assigned him a password, an email account and provided a copy of the employee handbook. Rebecca introduced him to a handful of his coworkers, looked at her watch, and said she'd be right back.

His immediate neighbour was a Hispanic woman who appeared to be a few years younger than him. "Hey, I'm Selena. I guess I'm your work buddy."

He sat in his chair; the previous owner's ass groove remained, but he was sure he could work in his own soon enough. "Hi, work buddy. I'm Jimmie."

She leaned into him and spoke in low tones. "I hear you're working with Gil."

"Yeah. I'm getting the sense that's not a good thing?"

"Gil is a character. He's...not everyone's cup of tea. Most people are happy you're here because it means we won't have to work with him. Listen, I don't want to scare you. He's been here longer than anyone else. He was a respected lawyer back in his day, but...you know what, maybe you'll have no problem with him. I shouldn't say too much. I didn't want you caught unaware."

"Thanks," he said as Rebecca returned.

"Ok, let's meet Gil."

Rebecca led him deeper into the back of the firm where the lawyers had their offices. They kept going down the main hallway past the offices. At the end of the hall, they turned and entered a narrower corridor near the bathrooms and a storage room. A lone office lay ahead; Loud voices emanated from behind the closed door. The voices coalesced into recognizable words as they got closer.

"....think I'm washed up. I know it, John, you and these snot-nosed punks, you think old Gil has lost a step. I have lost nothing, John, nothing. And Luther sends you, his lapdog, because he's too scared to talk to me."

"Luther thinks it's better for everyone if you have a special assistant, Gil. Someone you can work with and develop a rapport..."

"It's because none of those others want to work with me. Don't try to fool me, John. I know. You can't fool a fooler. I know."

"Gil, listen..."

"You stuck me away from everyone. By the shitters. Do you want to be near the shitters, John? You know John is another word for shitter, right?"

Jimmie and Rebecca stood there, not wanting to interrupt. "Listen," said John, his voice becoming agitated. "I'm not having this out with you. Luther wanted it this way. You don't like it, take it up with him. I'm done with this." The door abruptly opened, and John exited. He paused when he saw them standing there.

Gil peered around John. A white-haired man in his mid-70s, a scowl on his face as he stared at Jimmie. His tie hung loose, the top button on his shirt undone. His suit was twenty years out of date and hung on him, bigger than it should be, as if it were a relic from his younger, more robust days. "Holy shit. Is this the guy? What the hell is wrong with his hair?"

"Good talking to you, Gil. Jimmie," John looked at him. "Good luck." He strode past them and turned the corner.

"Goodbye. I'll leave you to get to know Gil," said Rebecca, retreating after John.

Jimmie stood in the hallway, not knowing what to do. Gil stood there, glowering at him. After what seemed like an eternity, Gil grunted. "So, what do they call you?"

"I'm Jimmie."

Gil grunted again. "Figures. Come in here." He turned and went into his office.

Gil's desk was a mess of piled papers and old coffee cups. A stale funk hung in the air; the room had no window. It was a former storage room converted into an office.

Gil threw himself into the well-worn chair. "So," he said. "Who did you piss off to get assigned to me, Jimmie?

You must have pissed someone off. Probably that prick Luther. You piss off Luther?"

"I have no idea what you are talking about. I just got hired. Today is my first day. I didn't know I would be assigned to you."

"Well, you're stuck with me, Jimmie, because none of the pukes who work here want to work with me. And I don't care. You know why? You know why I don't care? Because I shouldn't be here. I shouldn't be here. I should be on a boat, living the life, surrounded by twenty-year-olds in bikinis, enjoying the fruits of my fifty years of work. You know why I'm not? Because I got married. Three times. And not to women, no sir, not women. I got married to succubi, to three soul-sucking vampire spawn. These vampires are sucking me dry. They got their teeth into my ass, right in my ass, and they are acting like a pack of rabid dogs, and I'm wearing Milk-Bone underwear."

Jimmie stood there in silence.

"Listen to me, never get married, you hear me, never get married. Women want to get their hooks into you, and like Shylock, they want a pound of flesh from close to your heart. You know Shylock? William Shakespeare, Merchant of Venice, Shylock? A pound of flesh. Never get married, and they can't get the flesh from you. I was stupid, don't do what I did. But if your dick takes over from your brain and you get married, hide your assets from them, hide them. I wish I had. If I had, I wouldn't have to drag my sorry ass into this office, and sit by the shitters, and have you gaping at me like a moron."

Jimmie had no response.

"You a retard? Why are you standing there staring at me like a retard?" Jimmie opened his mouth to respond but thought better of it. It pained him, but he realized that sometimes, as much as you should speak up, you can't. He shook his head.

"They tried to tell me you were smart, boy. Told me you were a superstar, scored high on your exam. You know what? I don't give a fuck. Your pretty piece of paper doesn't mean jack-shit to me. Do as I tell you, and don't fuck up. You got that? Don't fuck up."

"I won't," said Jimmie, finding his voice. "It's my dream to work here. I want to help people. I will not screw this up."

"Jesus, you sound like Luther's old man. He was an idealist, like you. Gave me my start, back when I still cared about things, before I got involved with the hags. He was a good guy if naïve, not like his kid, not like Luther. Luther's not naïve, but he's not a good guy. Oh, he enjoys helping people; it gets him hard, oh so hard. But what he really likes is making money, a lot of money. If he helps someone along the line, great, as long as he gets the money. He'd love to get rid of me, oh yeah, he would, but he can't. His old man, he gave me a contract so tight, as one of the people who helped him build this firm, that if Luther tried to get rid of me, he'd have to pay me a fuckton of money, and Luther, he doesn't want to give up that money, no siree. He's too cheap to get rid of me, and I can't afford to quit on my own, on account of the succubi. So he sticks me back by the shitters and gives me a reject from Lynyrd Skynyrd to work with me. He figures he can drive me out, but I'm too fucking stubborn for him." Gil sighed, his rant having drained him. He rubbed his bleary eyes and looked up.

"I got some things you could do for me. Might as well make use of you." Gil picked up random empty coffee mugs and looked inside, rejecting them one after another until he came across one that didn't turn him off. "I got a whole mess of papers that need filing." He gestured at a precarious pile on a chair by the door. "File that, but only those. Don't touch the ones on my desk, never touch the ones on my desk. I got a system. Don't fuck up my system, don't fuck it up." Gil opened a drawer at the bottom of his desk, took out a bottle of Jack Daniels and poured a generous amount into his recovered coffee cup. Jimmie glanced at the clock on the wall: 9:45 am. "You go file those and check back in with me. The best part for you, working with the guy they stuck by the shitters, is no one gives me any important work to do. I get the dregs, the shit no one else wants. Those Ivy League cocksuckers, big shots like John, give me the stuff they can't be bothered to do themselves. I usually get shitfaced and pass out around 3:30. Nothing for you to do after that. Take those files and put them somewhere; the poofy redhead will show you where they go. Maybe I'll have something else for you to do, or maybe I won't. I don't know. Fuck it." Gil drained the mug of Jack Daniels in one shot. Jimmie went over, carefully picked up the files from the chair and exited Gil's office. He could hear Gil pouring himself another drink.

Jimmie carried the files back to his work station. Selena looked at him. "So, how was Gil?"

"Gil is...a character, as you said. But I can handle him. I think we can develop a rapport."

Selena snorted. "Yeah, good luck with that. I'm not sure I'll like you much if you develop a rapport with Gil."

Rebecca came over. "Oh, it looks like Gil gave you work. Let me show you how our system works so you can get the filing done."

The filing took two hours. It was before lunch when he checked back in on Gil.

"Wow, you came back, um...what's your name again?"

"Jimmie."

"Right, Jimmie. I have something for you. It should be enough to keep you busy and out of my hair. I need you to do research on a case, find precedents we can use. Trying to get them to settle out of court. Get enough precedents, and they might. They gave me this," he pointed at the dust-covered computer sitting on his desk, clearly not in use. "Apparently, you can look things up on it. But I don't know how to use the goddamn thing." He stifled a burp. "You're a superstar, they tell me. Find me those precedents and get back to me tomorrow. I won't need you anymore today; I'm going to have a nap."

Jimmie picked up the file folder Gil had pushed towards him, and realizing he'd been dismissed, left the office. He didn't know why everyone didn't like Gil. Yes, he was obnoxious, but hey, so were his friends and Gil delegated jobs and most of the time, you weren't anywhere near him. This could work out well.

Jimmie went back to his work station and dropped off the file. He'd get to work on it right after lunch. He and Selena went to Bob Evans.

Afterwards, he spent his afternoon on his computer, compiling a list of cases which showed precedence to Gil's case, putting them in a binder with colour-coded tabs to make it easy for Gil to follow. He wrapped up before quitting time.

As he packed up his station, John came up to him. "So," John inquired. "How was your first day?"

"Great, I loved it. I'm happy to be here and doing interesting and important work."

"And no trouble with Gil?'

"He's colourful, but I'm not unsympathetic to his position. Gil's an old-school guy left behind in our current world. He's crass, yes, misogynistic, has a persecution complex, paranoid, uses language he shouldn't, he's a slob and a functioning alcoholic, but once you get past all that, he's all right."

John shook his head, and he smiled. "If you can handle Gil, you should end up being a productive addition to our office. Good night." He chuckled as he walked away.

#

That night he joined his friends over at Gator's. "So," said Rob as they stood on the deck, leaning on the railing, staring at the alligators. "How was the first day at your big fancy job?"

"It was all right. They have me working for this eccentric guy. He was an eye-opener, but nothing I can't handle. The people there are nice, the work is interesting, and they are paying me better than I ever imagined making. I can't complain."

"Watch out, boys, he's evolving," snickered Clint. "Before you know it, he'll be kicking his Diet Coke addiction and getting laid."

They laughed at that. "I'll never give up on the Diet Coke, but I wouldn't mind getting laid."

Troy Young

Chapter 11

Stacy Keibler was grey; he'd awakened later than the day before. Jimmie was soon on his bike, off to work. Fishing out a cigarette from his pack, he stuck it in his mouth and attempted to get his lighter to catch while trying to steer his bike with one hand.

He had to hustle more today than yesterday since he hadn't woken up as early. *Can't get into a habit of waking up later and later,* he thought. *I can't ever be late.* As he reflected on this, he started to dream of once again being able to afford a car. He'd never need to worry about being late then. He'd linger on the patio in the morning. Oh, and help his mother by driving her to places. And not having to rely on his friends to take him everywhere. But mainly his moment of solitude on the patio.

He coasted into the parking lot with five minutes to spare. No time for Bob Evans this morning. "Good morning, Kathy," he said as he hurried into the office.

"Good morning. You're fired up and ready to take on the world."

"Nah," he said, leaning in close and lowering his voice. "Just Gil."

"Oh, Jimmie," laughed Kathy. "You are such a scoundrel."

He whistled a tune and had a bounce in his step as he headed to his workspace. He was the first paralegal there. Might as well check in with Gil.

Gil had his feet up on the only patch of his desk clear enough for them, the binder in his hand, engrossed in it as Jimmie entered.

"Jeremy, you do this?" asked Gil, indicating the binder. "I mean, by yourself? The poofy redhead didn't help you?"

"Yeah, it was me. And my name is Jimmie."

"Hmmm, what?"

"Jimmie. My name is Jimmie."

"Oh. Whatever," said Gil, dismissively. "This is great work, Jimmie. And I don't mean for your first try. I mean, it's the work of a seasoned professional. Far better than the others working around here, like that Spic girl. You could teach her a thing or two."

"Her name is Selena, and you shouldn't call her that," finding the voice which had failed him yesterday.

"What? Oh shit, don't tell me you are one of those bleeding-heart liberal types, are you? You a fucking snowflake? Or maybe you're thinking with your dick and not your head. You got a thing for her?"

"No, people shouldn't be treated poorly, especially at work."

"Oh, spare me your PC bullshit. Wake up, man, and look around. Those people are desperate to take what we've built. There are two types of people: those who make and those who take. I had things until I got married, and those succubi and their lawyers got their hooks in me. I look around me, and I see people, most of who don't belong here, wanting to take the things that hard-working real Americans sacrificed for. They want shit like equal rights and equal pay and other shit. The world ain't equal; it never has been. There have always been people with more than others. Because they worked for it. They had a plan, they wanted things, and they worked hard for them. And lazy sons-a-bitches who want what you have without having to work for it. We need constant vigilance to guard against that shit."

Jimmie stood there, not wanting to antagonize Gil further. And their day had started well.

"We have rights in this country. The government is always wanting to take away your rights. I can't call someone a faggot without the HR bitch coming in here and telling me I can't talk like that anymore. They are taking guns from people; at the same time, they are letting in undesirables from shithole countries. We need to protect ourselves from these animals. I remember when a man could be a man. You could have a few drinks and drive home, and no one cared. If my mother mouthed off, she got reminded by my old man who was in charge. People knew their place. The country was a great place then. Now it's all gone to shit. It's the PC bullshit you said that ruined this great country." Gil sighed and tossed the binder onto a pile of papers, and reached into the drawer for his bottle of Jack.

"Go back up front to your girlfriends and see if they'll take you to get a dress fitting. I'm done with you for now. Check back in before lunch; maybe I'll have something for one of your delicate sensibilities."

Dismissed, he backed out of the door. *That could have gone better,* he thought. It was apparent to him why the others were happy; they now had a buffer between them and Gil.

Selena was at her desk when he got back. "Wow, you came back," she said with a smile. "I figured after you left here common sense would take hold, and you'd run screaming out of here to get away from that nasty old man. But," she said, leaning in, "I'm glad you didn't. And not because you dealing with him means I don't need to, but you and I will be friends. I mean, take a peek around," she said, glancing at the others at their stations. "Everyone is at least seven years older than us. They are married and have pictures of their kids, or if they aren't married, there're pictures of their cats wearing little hats or something. It's a very straight-laced place. I need someone who I can relate to around here."

113

"And you think you can relate to me?' a slight blush coming to his face.

"Yeah, I do. There is a vein of weirdness to you," she smirked. "I like weird." She smiled at him and turned back to her computer.

With no direction from Gil, Jimmie checked in with Rebecca to offer to help. "Why, thank you, Jimmie. The firm is in the middle of a growth spurt, and we don't have everyone we need in place. Mr. Monroe is always looking for go-getters; he'll see something in you he likes," she said with a smile. Her vote of confidence made him believe he was on the right track.

He went back to Gil's office before lunch. The Jack Daniels had helped take the edge off him, as Gil was calmer than the last time he had seen him.

"Jim, I got more papers for you to file," he said, indicating two large piles on the credenza.

"It's Jimmie."

"I realize that's what you call yourself. That's a little boy's name. You want to be a man? Well, then, you're Jim. I will do my best to take you under my wing and make a man out of you, Jim."

He gave a stifled but exasperated sigh and nodded. He hated the name Jim. People had been trying to shorten his name on him all his life.

"You're real twitchy, you know that Jim? Listen, I took a deeper look at your research, and we can win this. Hey, after you're done filing, come on back and have a drink with me, Jim."

Jimmie froze as he picked up the stack of papers. He wasn't sure if he wanted to sit around drinking at the office with Gil. He tried to figure if he could manage both stacks at once, so he didn't have to come back. But he didn't see how he could do it. Resigned to this fate, he blurted out a hesitant "Sure."

"Thatta boy, Jim. It'll put hair on your balls."

Jimmie groaned and left.

He took his time with the stack of filing, putting off Gil as long as possible. Lucky for him, when he returned for the second stack, Gil wasn't in his office. He grabbed the remaining papers and left.

He finished the filing at 3:34. Lingering around the front as long as possible, he realized he'd have to return to Gil. Plucking up his courage at 4:45, he returned to the back office.

The fates had decided he had suffered enough of Gil today. Gil was there, but slumped in his chair, snoring faintly, the bottle of Jack, one-third full, sitting on the desk with a grimy looking coffee mug still containing a portion of liquid.

Jimmie wasn't going to wake him; Gil would yell at him. Still, he didn't want Gil to think he hadn't come back as directed. He took a post-it note pad off the desk and wrote, "You were asleep" on it. He almost signed it 'Jimmie' but agonized over it. Finally, he wrote 'Jim' and stuck the note onto the bottle.

He was happier than he should have been as he headed to clock out. As he returned to his station, he heard Luther Monroe's voice. "How is the new guy working, Rebecca?"

"Jimmie? Oh, he's a peach, a real peach. He's so nice and sweet. Works hard too. Always asking if we need help. He's a real quick learner. You got yourself a good one there."

Jimmie hesitated, not wanting to stroll into the middle of their conversation. Curious to learn more, he flattened himself against the wall to listen.

"Uh-huh. And how's he doing with Gil?"

"Well, you'd have to ask Gil, but he's cleared more backlog for Gil in the past two days than most do in a week. He takes it in stride, never stressed out about having to work with him." Jimmie couldn't see her, but he imagined she glanced around since she paused and whispered: "Gil can be a handful."

"Well, keep an eye on him, will you?" *Wow,* thought Jimmie. Luther Monroe wanted Rebecca to keep an eye on him. He remembered what she had told him earlier in the afternoon. Luther Monroe had plans for Jimmie Mayfield!

115

Realizing the danger of being caught eavesdropping, Jimmie strode out of the hall. Luther and Rebecca both glanced up at him. The rest of the office lay empty; everyone had clocked out for the day.

Luther looked right at him and stiffened. "Oh, Mr. Mayfield, you're still here?" Rebecca gave Jimmie a smile and gave Luther a small nod. "You're salaried. We don't pay you extra for staying late."

"I was checking in with Gil. He'd asked me to before I left."

Luther narrowed his eyes. "And how do you find it working for Mr. Lemon?"

It was time to be diplomatic. "I'm learning a lot from Mr. Lemon. It takes time to adjust to each other's idiosyncrasies. I suppose we are doing as well as we can."

"That's good to know. Don't let me keep you, Mr. Mayfield. You have a good night. Rebecca," he said with a nod and ambled back towards his office.

"Goodnight, Jimmie," said Rebecca. She grabbed her oversized purse off the back of her chair and threw the strap over her shoulder. She rooted around in it, searching for her keys as she walked toward the front door.

Jimmie turned off his computer and straightened up his desk. He left the building and walked to a convenience store in the plaza next to the office, grabbed himself a sixteen oz. bottle of Diet Coke for the road, a pack of cigarettes and a package of beef jerky. He'd order in a pizza and watch a DVD or two. Things were coming together for him.

The next day was the same as the one before it. Bathroom. Frosted Flakes. Diet Coke. Dressed. Bike. Cigarette. Got to work five minutes early. Stopped at the front desk to say good morning to Kathy and went to check on Gil.

"Morning, kid. Got your note," he nodded to the chair, now empty of papers since they had been filed. Jimmie sat. "That was a nice touch. Thought you would stand up old Gil. I know I can be crotchety, but you came back, Jim. I said I would turn you into a man, Jim. Men face things head-on. So," he said, taking a folder from the ledge behind his desk. "I've

116

been working on this one for a while, Jim. An old friend of mine from my Lodge. Guy's getting divorced. He's watched me go through this three times. He saw firsthand what I had to go through, and he wanted to be protected. Smart man. Wished I'd been smart. But someone has to be the trailblazer, I guess.

"For years, I've been helping him move assets around, keep them off the books, hide it from the government; those leeches always want too much from hard-working Americans. Good thing we did, because his wife is leaving him. Her barracuda lawyer is trying to get half of what he has. Well, there's less there than she expects. On paper anyhow, Jim, on paper. Michelangelo had the Sistine Chapel, Leonardo Da Vinci had the Mona Lisa, Francis Ford Coppola had the Godfather, and Gil Lemon has this." He pointed to the file. "This is a masterpiece. Best work I have ever done. We're talking millions, Jim, millions his bitch wife won't be getting her hands on."

"This doesn't sound ethical, Mr. Lemon."

"Ethical? Ethical?" said Gil, his voice starting to rise. "Don't tell me about ethics, Jim. The government taxes you on every dollar you earn. Then they tax you when you go to buy things. This is the money you've kept AFTER you've paid taxes, Jim. And then after a lifetime of paying taxes to the government on everything you've earned and everything you've bought with what you've earned, they fucking charge you a death tax. Then if you have people you wanted to leave the money and shit you bought to, the stuff you've already paid taxes on, the government wants to take half of that too. The government is the biggest fucking racket going. Those black guys walking around with their asses hanging out of their pants think they're gangsters? The real fucking gangsters wear goddamn suits and live in Washington, Jim."

"And his wife?"

"Holy shit, boy, I thought I was getting through to you. His wife is a succubus! They all are. They take and take and take; the succubi are never satisfied. She'll come out all right. I mean, we couldn't hide the fucking house, Jim. That's on the books. Although we took out a huge fucking mortgage on it a few years back and funnelled the equity offshore. She'll have debts on that fucking house. But we couldn't hide everything; she'll get a few million bucks. I'd have tried to leave her with nothing, but my buddy said he should keep a few scraps to throw her way. Soft-hearted idiot that he is."

"So why are you telling me this?"

"I got the paperwork here. I want you to fax it to him. It's got a list of everything he's got out of reach of the bitch, and the papers we're turning over to her lawyers. I want you to send it to him so he can see how it's laid out. I need him to sign the papers, and we will send them to the succubus' lawyer." Gil glanced at the file's cover page, scrawled a fax number on a post-it note, and affixed it to the file's front. "Fax the whole package over to him at this number and wait for his response. I'll call him and tell him it's coming." Gil leaned towards him. "The firm is involved only in the divorce; I've been freelancing on the other stuff, Jim. I'll kick you over a small bonus for keeping this quiet, you got that? You do this for me, and I'll look after you, Jim. We'll make a hell of a team."

Jimmie hesitantly took the file. Gil had admitted to him he'd committed a crime. He should go tell Luther Monroe at once. What if Gil was lying? What if this was a test? In fact, he wondered if Gil was another part of an extended interview. Put people into crazy situations and see how they react? No contract could be iron-clad enough to keep a guy like this around, could it? What did they want Jimmie to do? Tell the boss about the criminal acts of one of his lawyers? Or follow orders? What if Gil was telling the truth? Maybe he was a terrible old man who wasn't part of innovative hiring practices. Jimmie began to sweat; his pulse began to race. If he faxed it as Gil had asked, did that make him an accessory to a crime?

"Why are you still here?" Gil growled. "Go send that, will you?"

He got up out of the chair and nodded at Gil. As he passed Luther's door, he paused. He could hear Luther talking on the phone. Jimmie reached out to knock on it but stopped himself; he didn't know what to do.

He told me to fax this, so I should fax it, he thought. *If it was as Gil said, well, nothing will happen. The divorce will be settled, and the guy will keep his money. The wife is getting a few million out of it. I'm not a party to any details. I'm just sending a fax.*

He'd send the fax and deny Gil said anything to him if it went sideways. That's part of his job, right? Do your job. He hurried over to the fax machine, loaded the files into the hopper, and punched in the fax number on the post-it note. The pages started to feed themselves through the scanner; once they had gone through, the machine began to dial—the device connected to the other fax and began transmission. Jimmie gathered up the files and put them back into the folder. He ripped the post-it off the front of the folder and fed it through the shredder by the fax.

"Here," he said, handing the file back to Gil. "I faxed it to the number you gave me."

"I told him to call me when he got it. Go back to the machine and wait for his return fax."

Jimmie sweated as he reached the fax. Selena was using the shredder. "Whoa. You look whiter than normal. And you're clammy too. You feeling sick?"

"What? No, no. Sick? Me? I don't get sick. I'm fine. Fine. Just waiting for a fax for Gil. Nothing strange about that. Nope, nothing strange. Just getting a fax for old Gil."

"Ok," said Selena, rolling her eyes.

Jimmie stared impatiently at the fax. Nothing. Who uses faxes these days? Couldn't we email it? He realized Gil didn't want to leave an electronic trail. Emails reside on servers and can be recovered. Attorney-Client privilege doesn't count if the lawyer is part of a crime. Gil thought ahead. And then he realized no, Gil wasn't thinking ahead. Gil probably didn't know there was even a thing called email. Gil never turned on his computer, he didn't own a cell phone. He sat in the back in his office, slowly dying. It surprised Jimmie

Gil knew what a fax was. Speaking of faxes, where the fuck was that fax?

It had been 15 minutes since he sent the fax. Should have gotten it, read it and signed the page. Maybe the old fart didn't know how his fax worked. Gil didn't know how to use this fax. That's why he brought Jimmie into this. He was now party to a crime because the old racist drunk they forced him to work for didn't know how to use a fucking fax machine!

Something was wrong. Jimmie sweated profusely. He needed a cigarette, but he dared not leave the fax machine.

Then he heard it. Not the fax, but the sheer unbridled fury that was Gil, coming from the hallway.

"WHERE THE FUCK IS THAT LOSER! THE LITTLE SHIT WITH THE STUPID HAIR! YOU'VE FUCKING RUINED ME, YOU SON OF A BITCH! I'M GOING TO KILL HIM!"

Gil entered the room. "YOU DUMBASS! YOU FAXED IT TO THE WRONG PLACE! YOU FUCKING FAXED IT TO THE SUCCUBUS' LAWYER!"

By now, Gil's screams had brought out everyone in the office. Luther came over and approached Gil, speaking calmly. "Now Gil, you can't be carrying on this way. This is a place of business. What is the matter?"

"Fuck off, Luther, you smug son of a bitch. I'm fucking ruined, don't you get it, ruined. This piece of shit you hired faxed a very sensitive divorce file to my client's wife's lawyer. There were details in the file not meant for them. I got off the phone with her lawyer. He thanked me for the great details and said the fucking Feds would be happy to see it. Hoped my client and I liked the fucking food in prison."

Gil turned on Jimmie. "If I'm going to prison, it might as well be for something worthwhile. I'll kill that punk." Gil lunged at him. Lucky for Jimmie, security had arrived, and they subdued him.

Luther looked Gil right in the eye. "If you have jeopardized this firm, the Feds will be the least of your worries."

"Don't worry, your precious firm is safe. I should have made sure that if I went down, I'd take you with me. I've hated working here the last fifteen years, you pompous ass. You and these pukes. Go to hell, Luther!" Gil spat at him.

Luther wiped the spittle off his face. "Your illegal actions have nullified your contract with this firm. I've been dreaming of being able to rid myself of you for years. Get him out of here. But not through reception. I don't want to see him on the property ever again. And fumigate that disgusting office of his. After you've gone through his files to see what else is worrisome to the firm."

Security began to drag Gil away. "I should have left a big steaming coil in my bottom desk drawer for you. One more piece of shit to go with the pieces of shit who work here. I'll see you in hell, in..." Security had taken him out of the room.

Everyone stood for a few tense moments. "Mr. Mayfield," said Luther.

"Yes, sir?"

"You're fired. Get your things and go."

"But sir, I had nothing to do with it. He asked me to fax the files to his client. Just send a fax. He wrote the number on a post-it note. It wasn't my fault."

"Mr. Monroe," began Rebecca, hesitantly. "Jimmie hasn't been here long enough to be involved. This is Gil's fault."

"Regardless of whether he was involved with this unseemly case," said Luther, "he has shown a lack of judgment and mishandled legal documents. What if he shared other files with the wrong office? We can't have these types of mistakes."

"But Jimmie said Gil gave him the number on a post-it," said John, who had been observing the scene with the rest of the crowd.

Luther did not turn from Jimmie. "Do you have this post-it note still, son?" he asked.

"No, sir. I shredded it."

121

"Then we have no proof you didn't make this mistake. I'm sorry, but I cannot be sure you didn't do this. I'm not comfortable giving you a second chance. You can either get your things and leave," Luther narrowed his eyes, "or you can go out like Gil."

Jimmie slumped, and his knees felt weak. His time and energy wasted. He'd never get another job as a paralegal. Other firms would hear of this. He felt lost. He began to cry. He realized he had nothing to gather. He couldn't even make eye contact with anyone. He turned and left.

Chapter 12

Leaving the cool embrace of the Monroe Group's air-conditioned environs and stepping out into the hot, muggy Florida air, Jimmie gazed at the sky. The clouds were as dark as his mood; in the distance, a flash of lightning and a peal of thunder announced the incoming storm.

He felt empty. He wasn't angry. He wasn't even sad. Just empty. Defeated. He had been unfairly denied his chance to change his circumstances. They shattered his plan; he had nothing else.

It was still morning. The morning of only his third day. Brought low through no fault of his own. *Well, not entirely no fault,* he thought. He'd had a chance, when he lingered at Luther's door, to extricate himself from this mess. If he knocked and told Luther what he'd discovered. Or John. Or even Rebecca. Hell, even Selena could have advised him. Any of them would have acted. He didn't, and now he was paying the price.

What would he do? He couldn't stand here; he had to go somewhere. He didn't want to go home as he might run into his mother, and she'd ask why he wasn't at work. The emotional toll of dealing with her inevitable breakdown was too much to handle. She'd be crushed. He needed time to come to grips with this himself before he submitted her to this.

He thought about Rob. Rob would mock him, tell him yet again Jimmie was incapable of keeping a job. For all he knew, his friends had a pool going. Rob likely had picked he'd be fired within a week. He would not go see Rob and give him the satisfaction.

Clint? While Clint could cut through and analyze human nature, this wasn't in his bailiwick. Besides, he couldn't disturb him at work.

Ryan. He would go to Ryan. Ryan was the practical one of the group. Quiet and not judgemental. He'd let him pour it out and listen. Clint and Rob would offer advice, and he didn't need that right now. He needed sympathy, and Ryan was the best to provide it.

Jimmie unlocked his bike as the first drops of rain began to fall. *Great,* he thought. *Just what I need. I hope at least the lightning holds off until I get there. Can't ride in that.*

He started to pedal towards Play Bowl! to see Ryan. When a Florida rain comes on, it often comes on fast and hard and violent. This one was no exception. He wasn't out of the parking lot, and it soaked him. Lucky for him Play Bowl! was near his office...former office, he caught himself. In less than twenty minutes, he pulled into the parking lot of Play Bowl! He'd had to remove his tie and use it as a headband to help keep the water from running into his eyes. His dress shoes squished as he walked, and his dress shirt stuck to his skin, so you saw his nipples and sparse chest hair through the thin fabric. His hair hung dripping over his shoulders.

Jimmie shivered as the air conditioning of Play Bowl! assaulted his soaking clothes and skin. He wandered through the flashing lights of the arcade towards the sounds of balls colliding with pins. As it was mid-morning and midweek, the only people playing were seniors in their league play. It was still early for the snowbirds; in two weeks, they'd pack the alley to capacity.

Ryan was giving two old ladies bowling shoes. He chatted with them, counting out their change when his eyes alighted on Jimmie. Ryan finished with his customers and came over to him.

The (Extra)ordinary Life of Jimmie Mayfield

"What are you doing here? You're dripping! Why aren't you at work? Is something wrong? No one died, did they?"

Jimmie shook his head, his teeth chattering; damn Florida's obsession with overly air-conditioned places. "No. I got fired. I needed to talk to someone. Do you have time to talk?"

Ryan looked at his watch. "I'm not scheduled for my break for another twenty-three minutes, but I can get someone to cover me. It's not that busy. Why don't you head into the bar, and I'll join you in a few minutes? I need to find my manager."

Jimmie squished his way into the empty bar. He eased his way into a booth.

Five minutes later, Ryan came in, holding a pink hoodie. "Here; I got it from lost and found. You looked cold. This should help." Ryan handed it over as he sat opposite him.

"Thanks," Jimmie said, pulling on the hoodie. The woman who owned it was more abundant than he; it hung on him and the excess pooled on the bench around him. It smelled of stale cigarette smoke and cheap perfume. Still, it helped protect him from the air conditioning.

"So, what happened?" asked Ryan.

"Well," he began, having struggled to lay it out in his head on the ride. "I told you about the eccentric guy they had me working with? I miscategorized him. I should have told you they had me working for a misogynist, racist, drunken criminal. He'd been working on a divorce case and had been trying to hide assets from the government and the guy's wife on the chance they ever got divorced. He told me about it, I'm not sure why, I think he wanted to brag to me, to show me how smart he was, sticking it to both 'The Man' and 'The Succubi.'"

"The succubi?" Ryan looked confused.

"Never mind. He told me to fax the papers over to his client for review before we faxed the doctored file to the wife's lawyer. I guess he looked at the top page, the file for the wife, and scrawled her lawyer's fax number by mistake."

"Oh, so..."

"So yeah, now the wife knows everything this guy's been hiding. Her lawyer said he'd turn it over to the Feds to investigate the hidden assets."

"They're screwed then. The government doesn't appreciate it when people don't give it the money they owe. But that doesn't explain why you got fired?"

"No, it doesn't. Luther Monroe didn't care. Gil, that's the guy I worked with, insists I screwed up, not him. Luther didn't even listen to me. Said I had 'shown a lack of judgment and mishandled legal documents,' and he would not give me a second chance. I should have gone to him; I should have told someone. Why did I shred the damn post-it note that had the fax number? The proof I sent it to where Gil told me to send it. I screwed up. It might not be fair, but I caused this. It's my fault."

Ryan shook his head. "It doesn't seem that way to me. Don't be hard on yourself."

Jimmie stared at the table, not willing to look at Ryan. He gave a dejected shrug.

"Did they give you an orientation on what to do if you discovered something illegal?"

"No."

"Did they show you a policy on whistleblower protection?"

He sat up straighter and looked Ryan in the eye. "No, they did not."

"They failed you. Most professional places orient their employees to these kinds of things. It doesn't sound like a great office to work in, Jimmie."

He sat there, stunned. "They gave me an employee handbook, but it was limited and grossly out of date. I saw a date in it; it said 1987."

"A big firm should have up-to-date HR policies."

He shook his head and screwed up his face. "Where did you learn so much about Human Resources?"

"Gus who worked here skimmed money from the token machine in the arcade. A teenage employee named

126

Betsy found out, and he agreed to include her to keep her quiet. They got caught and fired. We had a half-day session to make sure it didn't happen again." Ryan leaned in and lowered his voice. "This place is a soap opera. You wouldn't believe the stuff that goes on around here."

"Well, maybe you're right, but I'm still fired."

"You can't go apply at another firm? You got great marks, didn't you?"

"I doubt it would work. I'm sure it will get around they fired me on my third day. Who'd want to hire me?"

"Yeah, well, you can't give up that easy. People might hear you were unfairly treated in this affair. They might not hold it against you."

"I guess. I can look up other places, send them my resume and grades. I might get an interview. But you know, it wasn't doing the job. It was doing it *there*. Luther Monroe was a larger-than-life person. He'd inspired me to want to do this. And now he's the dickhead who fired me."

"They say we should never meet our heroes," said Ryan, looking at his watch. "I hate to do this, but I have to get back to work."

"Thanks for listening to me. Could you do me another favour?"

"Sure. What is it?"

"Can you tell Rob how it happened? Otherwise, he'll lay into me for screwing up another job. Call me a loser or something."

"I can do that. My brother isn't a bad person, but he can sometimes be insensitive. He means well, but his 'tough love' routine gets stale. If either of us talked to him like he talks to us, he'd lose his mind." Ryan patted Jimmie on the shoulder. "I'll convince him so when he sees you, not to bug you."

"Thanks." He indicated the pink hoodie. "Should I give this back to you, or keep it? I mean, it's not my style, but I've become attached to this scent. I wished I knew what it was."

Ryan looked at him funny, and Jimmie gave him a laugh. "Nah, I'm messing with you," he said, taking off the hoodie. He looked at Ryan. "Thanks. I had nowhere else to turn."

"What are you going to do now?"

"I'll drive around for a while if the rain has stopped. Sneak home and get changed into something more me. Go to Gator's, see if Myrna's working. I..." he stood there, contemplating things for a few seconds. "I think she'd understand. She'll make me feel better. I don't know, I've been thinking about her since the wrestling show. She's so grounded, so supportive, so understanding."

Ryan gave him a faint smile. "We'll catch up to you there later. I got to go."

"Yeah, me too."

#

Ryan watched Jimmie leave and called his brother. "What do you want?" asked Rob gruffly after they had tracked him down on the docks.

"It's Jimmie. He got fired today."

"What? For fuck's sake, what is wrong with that boy?"

"Shut up. This was not his fault. Listen, call Clint. Ask him to get you after work. We need to discuss this. He needs us."

"What he needs is a swift kick in the keister."

"No, he doesn't. I'll explain it to you when I see you. And what are you, seventy? Who says keister?"

"Fine. I'll agree to withhold my judgment until you've filled me in on what happened. Clint is picking me up anyhow. Where should we meet? At Gator's?"

"No, he's going there. Come here first. We can talk at the bar here before we go see him."

"Right, well, I get off at two. What time are you done?"

"Three. See you around then." He hung up the phone.

#

The rain had stopped when Jimmie went back outside to get his bike. Rainfall in Florida will often linger for days or be short and heavy. Today the rain was shortlived. The sun breaking through the clouds helped to improve his mood.

He went for a long ride on his bike. The sun and wind dried the remaining moisture from his clothes, although his cheap dress shoes still squished, and as they started to dry, they grew uncomfortable. The rain ruined his pack of cigarettes. There were two salvageable ones. He smoked both on his ride.

At two o'clock, he got back to the trailer park. He had barely made it in when he heard a horn. He stopped and looked up. Chester. His heart sank. But at least his mother wasn't in the car with him.

Chester rolled down the window. "Hey, man," he said with a smile. "What's up? You're home early."

"Yeah. Where's my mom?"

"She's having a nap over at my place. She...um...hit her medicine hard. She's dozy right now. I'm going to get munchies."

"Thanks." Jimmie hesitated and then said, "Look, Chester, please don't tell her, but I got fired today. Unfairly fired," he added, seeing the look appearing on Chester's face. "It wasn't my fault. It was a bad situation I got tied up in. I'll tell my mom; she needs to hear it from me. This will hurt her."

Chester sighed. "Ok, I believe you. I got your back with your mom. But you have to tell me the details, ok? Not now, when you're ready. I don't want to see her hurt either, but I'll be better able to help manage this if I got something to work with, all right?"

He nodded. Chester rolled up the window and drove out of the park without another word.

Jimmie changed his clothes. A clean tank top and a mostly fresh pair of lounge pants. He slipped into his flip flops and got out of the park without seeing his mom.

#

He took his time getting to Gator's. The six o'clock news came on the TV as he walked into the bar. The tourists who gawked at the alligators had thinned, and the regulars had not arrived. Myrna was clearing away tables. "Hey, Jimmie," she said with a slight smile. "You're here early."

"Yeah. I want to talk to you."

"Oh," she said, perplexed. "Ok, I guess. What is it?" She smoothed an errant hair off her face, tucking it behind her ear, her left hand planted on her hip.

"Can I sit? It's not a short thing."

"Of course. Come over to the bar. Can I get you a drink?"

"Yeah, that might help."

She handed him a Yuengling. "Here you go. Now, what is it?"

"You remember we were in here on Monday night, celebrating my job?"

"Yeah. You got hired to work at that billboard guy's place, right?"

"Right. Well, I started Monday, and they fired me this morning."

"What? Three days in? What did you do?"

"Why do you think I did something?"

"You said fired. Not laid off, or let go, declared surplus or a different term; fired implies something happened. I'm not trying to be hard on you, just honest."

"Yeah. Well, I got blamed for something. Something I didn't do. Well, I did it, but only because the guy I reported to told me to do it."

"And he shouldn't have?"

"No. The guy did something illegal. You don't need the details. I got caught up in the shuffle."

"Do they know this? That he did illegal things?"

"Oh, yeah, they found out. Guy lost his mind and started swearing at everyone. They fired him too."

130

"Wow. I'm sorry. I don't know what to say. Beer's on me."

"Thanks. I didn't come for charity, though."

"Why did you come here?"

Jimmie drew in a deep breath. "I thought you'd understand. I enjoy talking to you. You cut through the crap and make sense of things. You're patient, and you're kind and the nicest person I know. I watched you with the residents of St. Alban's at the wrestling match. You never lost your cool with anyone. I figured I needed a shoulder to cry on, and yours would be a good one. Sorry."

"Sorry? Why say sorry?" Myrna put her hands on his shoulders. "You're a sweet guy and smart." She came around the bar and pulled him in for a comforting hug. "You can always come cry on my shoulder if you need it."

Jimmie sat there, enjoying her warmth. He awkwardly hugged her back and took a sniff of her hair. It smelled of a mix of sweat and the same scent which lingered on the pink hoodie earlier. He was about to ask her what it was when his eye caught something on the TV. He pulled away from her abruptly. "Myrna, can you turn up the sound?"

"Yeah, sure, why? I'll even back it up," she said, breaking off the hug and grabbing the remote. She rewound it and turned up the sound.

The newscast was ending, and the local anchor said, "well folks, only in Florida does this happen. Late this afternoon, three men arrived at a local business in Port Charlotte. They threw a live alligator through the front doors. As you can see from the security footage here..." the screen shifted from the anchor to grainy black and white footage of three men carrying an alligator across a parking lot. The three of them wearing dark clothes and ape masks. "... the three men appear carrying a five-foot alligator up to the front doors of the law offices of the Monroe Group before 5:00 pm today..." The footage changed to show the front doors of the office, the three men and their squirming package appearing at the bottom of the screen. The double doors slide open as they approach, and they heave the animal into the waiting room.

The three men then turn and run, the largest of the group hitting a shorter man with a potbelly and knocking him to the ground. The third man helps him up, and they run out of the shot. Moments after them, panicked people come pouring out of the doors, tripping over each other in their attempt to escape. "... and as you can see, they throw the alligator through the open doors into the packed lobby."

Now the screen showed the flustered visage of Luther Monroe. "These reprobates who perpetrated this travesty today on the Monroe Group, the third-largest firm in the state of Florida, will be brought to justice because that's what the Monroe Group does; justice. These degenerates didn't just terrorize us, no sir, they terrorized the fine people who turned to the Monroe Group in their time of need. People come to the Monroe Group when they have exhausted all avenue of hope because we care. We care, we really do. And these people, already at the lowest point in their lives, as they turn to the Monroe Group for help, and help they get, as we are right there beside them all the way, these poor people have terrorists, law enforcement might not want to call them that, but that's what they are, terrorists, commit this act of incredible indecency upon them. We at the Monroe Group will not rest until we bring these men to justice. Until the police have rounded them up, and the full authority of the law comes down hard upon them, we will not rest. We are fighters at the Monroe Group. We fight for you, and we will fight these evildoers. And," said Luther, now looking into the camera, "the Monroe Group wins most of its cases. We helped thousands get millions they otherwise wouldn't have received. These men will pay for their deeds."

The screen moved back to the anchor. "The alligator in question had its jaws duct-taped together, so it posed minimal risk to the people in the lobby. Still, it is a felony in Florida for people to interfere with alligators. The local ASPCA is advocating animal cruelty charges be added to any charges levied on these men because of the duct tape on the jaws."

Jimmie stared wide-eyed at the screen, his mouth open in disbelief.

"Was that...." Myrna began, turning to face him.

"Nope. We do not know those people." It was apparent to both of them they had watched Clint, Rob, and Ryan throw an alligator through the office's front doors.

Myrna started to howl. Her nose wrinkled up and her eyes narrowed, tears streaming from them, and she had to hold on to her stomach to prevent herself from doubling over in laughter. Jimmie started to laugh too, and the two of them sat at the bar laughing, drawing looks from the few patrons and staff who were there.

Troy Young

Chapter 13

Rob, Ryan and Clint showed up at Gator's, sauntering over to where Jimmie camped out at the bar. Rob gave him a nod. "Hey man, Ryan told us what happened. Sorry to hear about it. Dumbass dickhead was lucky to have you there."

"Yeah, sorry, bud," said Clint, clapping his meaty hand onto Jimmie's neck and giving him a friendly shake.

"We saw you on the news."

The three men stood there with blank expressions on their faces. "I don't know what you're talking about," said Clint.

Myrna walked over and placed three beers in front of them. "On the house, boys," she said with a smile.

"Myrna has never given me a free beer in my life," said Clint.

"Me neither," said Rob.

"I've gotten a few," said Ryan.

Rob playfully punched his brother as he took a long swig on his beer.

"Well, somebody threw an alligator through the front doors of the Monroe Group this afternoon. Myrna and I saw it on the news."

"That's strange," said Clint. "I hadn't heard. Had you Rob?"

Rob shook his head. "Nope. I think I'd remember hearing that. Ryan?"

Ryan looked uneasy. He couldn't face Jimmie. "Nooooo...."

"Thanks, fellas."

They stood and nodded in silence, sipping their beers.

"Let's get a booth," suggested Clint. I got something I want to run by you."

They secured a booth. "It sucks you got screwed over. I know you wanted it. I have something, while not working at a law office, might be up your alley."

"What do you have?"

"Big Sonny has an opening he needs to fill. It's a...different gig, but he needs someone reliable," said Clint.

"What, come work with you? Why didn't you offer him something before now?" asked Rob.

"It's not with me. C'mon, being a mechanic is a special skill. You can't take anyone off the street and make them a mechanic. It's not pumping gas at a marina."

"Hey, watch it."

Clint continued, ignoring Rob. "It's the courtesy driver. The guy who drives people around when they drop their car off to get work done."

"How is that different?" asked Ryan.

"Because it's for Big Sonny. It's not a nine-to-five gig. Big Sonny has... expectations. You are on call in the evenings; you'll get a cell phone and a pager..."

"They still make pagers?" said Rob.

"Yes," said Clint.

"Why a pager? That's stupid."

"Because sometimes he sends you a phone number, and he expects you to call back from a random landline. He wants you to always be in contact."

"Sounds sketchy," said Ryan.

"Big Sonny likes to entertain, all right? He needs someone who can be discrete, run errands, and pick up VIPs. Someone who knows how to keep his mouth shut and look the other way. Don't worry," said Clint, seeing the expression on

Jimmie's face. "He won't ask you to do illegal shit. He gets into grey areas, but never outright illegal stuff. Big Sonny imagines himself as a wiseguy, but keeps his business legit."

"So why is this job available?"

"Because the guy doing this for Big Sonny got picked up in the Everglades with ten kilos of cocaine in the trunk of his car."

"I don't know."

"You got any immediate options? I told Big Sonny this afternoon I might have a guy for him. Big Sonny is a character, a big mouth jerk, but he's a decent guy. Salt of the earth. He started as a mechanic at a dealership in New Jersey. Married the owner's daughter and inherited the dealership. He owns four dealerships in Newark and another three here. The guy's set. You get in his good books, and he'll take care of you. He is loyal to his people. Well, loyal to everyone but his wife," snickered Clint. "That's part of the reason you're on-call in the evenings, and he needs someone with discretion."

"Doesn't sound too bad," said Rob. "Shit, if he doesn't want it, maybe put in a word for me."

"No," said Clint, shaking his head. "Besides, how are you going to be a courtesy driver when you lost your license to a DUI?"

"Ah, shit, right. I hate this."

"I mean, it's not working in a law office, but it's something to do while you send out resumes to other firms. It might be temporary, or you might end up liking it," said Ryan.

"What's the pay?"

"Thirty-five thousand a year. Plus, other perks and bonuses. When he's done something that makes him feel guilty, he might give you a couple extra bucks as a thank you. Oh, and you get to take the car home with you. You can use it evenings and weekends, as long as you don't go crazy with it."

"Well, shit. That's better than my gig," said Rob.

"Mine, too," said Ryan.

"What do you say? If you're interested, he wants to meet you tomorrow."

"Tomorrow? This is quick. I need time to ruminate on this."

"That's not how it works in the real world. You sometimes need to be bold and grab hold of the opportunities when they present themselves."

"Yeah, I've learned what happens when you don't act at once," said Rob.

Clint gave Rob a sideways glance. "It's up to you, but you pass on this, and it's the last time I offer you help. You're on your own."

Jimmie sat silently, peeling the label off of his beer bottle. It would be simple to say no, to resume his routine. But as Clint said, did he have any immediate options? Being a dancing pancake again didn't sit well with him. If he had another job lined up would take the sting out of admitting he'd been fired to his mother. "All right, I'll go see him tomorrow."

"That's great. I'll tell him you are dropping by the lot. He's shooting a commercial tomorrow morning. If he likes you, you'll start right away. Two minutes after he says you're hired, you'll start, so have your license on you. Big Sonny works fast, and he expects you to. When he tells you to jump, you jump and think later. Listen, you call people out when they say and do stupid things; I admire that. But with Big Sonny, you bite your tongue. He doesn't appreciate being contradicted, especially around people. I'm not saying you don't bring it up with him, just not in the heat of the moment. He's malleable, but he'll harden up if you challenge him. I put myself out there for you, I'm vouching for you, and if you mess up, it looks bad on me. At least wait until you and he have felt each other out and have developed your own thing before you go all social justice warrior on him."

"I hate that term," said Jimmie.

"This is the shit I'm talking about. You hate it? Fine. If Big Sonny says something similar, you let it lie. You can tell him later why that term isn't one to use. You might convince him. But play it smart, ok?"

"Ok."

"Attaboy."

138

They sat there for a few minutes. "So, we made the news, huh?" asked Rob.

"I thought we weren't going to discuss it!" hissed Ryan.

"What? C'mon, he said it was on the news."

"Yep. Complete with security footage. Did it hurt when Clint knocked you over, Rob?"

"Ah, shit. On camera?"

"Yep. Saw you coming across the parking lot. Saw you throw the alligator through the front doors. You guys tripping over yourselves and people running out of the office. The ape masks were a nice touch."

"Thanks," said Ryan.

"I wanted a Joker mask," said Rob.

"They both wanted to be the Joker," added Clint.

"No. I said we could have more than one Joker," said Ryan.

"Criminal masterminds they aren't," said Clint.

"And you are? I'd call this more a prank than a crime," said Rob.

"They said on TV it's a felony to interfere with an alligator. ASPCA wants animal cruelty charges added too. And man, Luther was pissed."

Both Rob and Ryan blanched. Clint sipped his beer.

"Ah, fuck," said Rob.

Troy Young

Chapter 14

"Look at these beauties! You got a family? You need an SUV? We've got SUVs. This Dodge Journey: manufacturer wants you to cough up twenty-three large for this. Big Sonny will put you in one for eighteen. Eighteen!

"Don't have a family? Want luxury? We got this 300S—tons of power, tons of luxury. Big Sonny'll put you in one for only forty large. Forty! Other guys, they want forty-three.

"But no, I know what you want. You're a muscle guy. We got the best muscle right here! We got the Challenger SXT. The guys in Detroit, they want thirty large from you to get behind the wheel of this. Big Sonny'll do it for twenty-five! Twenty-five! Can you fucking believe it?"

"CUT!" yelled the director.

Big Sonny rolled his eyes, exasperated. Behind him, the inflatable men flapped their arms in the breeze while the giant gorilla on the roof loomed over everything. "Cut? Why cut? I was on a roll!"

"You can't use profanity in a commercial, Sonny."

"What'd I say?"

"You said, 'can you fucking believe it'."

"No, I didn't."

The director motioned over to the monitor. "Can you play that back so Sonny can see it?"

Big Sonny approached the monitor. '...wheel of this. Big Sonny'll do it for twenty-five! Twenty-five! Can you fucking believe it?' Sonny shrugged. "So, can't you guys take that out in, what do you call it, post?"

"No," said the director.

"Hey, back in Jersey, we'd bleep it before we aired it. Bleep it."

"This isn't New Jersey, Sonny. It's implied. People will consider it, and you, to be crass."

"I am crass. But I know how to fucking sell cars. Maria," he yelled. A young woman, well dressed in a navy suit with Gucci sunglasses on nodded. "Yeah, Dad?"

"Can you tell Mr. Fancy Director your old man knows how to sell cars?"

"My dad knows how to sell cars," said Maria. "What he doesn't know is how to go two minutes without dropping an f-bomb. Dad, listen to the director, and do it again."

"Bah," said Big Sonny. He turned to the director. "Your daughter talk to you this way?"

The director shook his head. "No, she's six."

"You have something to look forward to then. Fine. We'll do it again. But let's take ten, all right? I need to build it back up again."

The director nodded. "Take ten, everyone."

Jimmie had been watching the proceedings, fascinated. He'd never watched a commercial being filmed. He'd been watching Big Sonny to get a sense of the type of guy he was. Even after observing Sonny, he was still unsure.

Last night after the bar, he'd told his mother he lost his Monroe Group job. As expected, it had upset her. What had not been expected was how she tore into him, exasperated. "You have to change. I think it's my fault. I've coddled you too much. I've looked the other way when you made mistakes. I've made you a mama's boy. Well, Mama needs to work on her. Mama can't worry about her little baby bird no more. You're a grown man, so act like one. Start accepting responsibility. And for gosh sakes, get married and give me a grandchild!" It went off the rails then.

Telling her he had something else lined up, and the Monroe Group ended up not being what he'd expected it to be, mollified her. He would still apply to other law firms. He accepted her charge; it was time to act like an adult.

Jimmie filled Chester in over a round of drinks on what had transpired at the Monroe Group. Chester proved sympathetic. "Doesn't sound like a good environment for you. It was only a matter of time before it blew up. Luther is a real dickhead. I always thought so, watching him on the TV with his stupid 'Fighting for You' and his puppy-dog eyes. I can help calm your mom, but," he admonished. "Don't mess this next one up. One more strike, and she's liable to kick you out."

Jimmie was determined to get this job.

Santino 'Big Sonny' Delvecchio came over. "Hey, you. You the guy Clint mentioned? He said I'd recognize you on account of the hair." Jimmie was not a tall man, shorter than average, but Big Sonny barely came up to his shoulder.

"Yes, sir."

"Sir? I'm no goddamn sir. Queen never knighted me. Call me Big Sonny. Everyone does." Sonny leaned in close. "It's because my dick is so big," he said, laughing loudly. "I'm just fucking with you. You need a sense of humour around me, boyo. You got to keep up with me. I'm like the fucking Energizer bunny." Sonny looked at him. "You're twitchy. You a nervous type, boy? I don't like twitchy people; they make me feel weird. Grow a set, and calm down, all right? The big lummox who fixes cars for me says I can depend on you. That you're a good guy. That right?"

Jimmie took a deep breath, determined to convince Big Sonny he was the guy for the job. "That's right," he said with a confidence he didn't have.

"Clint tell you what I needed?"

"He said you need a courtesy driver."

"I got three. What I need, they can't do."

"He said I'd be your go-to guy, your fixer. That I'd be on call. That I'd run errands and stuff for you, whatever you needed, whenever you needed. And I needed to keep my mouth shut."

"And this appeals to you, does it? You think you're up for the job?"

"I do."

"Fine. You're hired. Maria!"

She was talking to the director. "Yes, Dad?"

"Take this... um... hey kid, what's your name?"

"Jimmie Mayfield."

"Jimmie Mayfield. I had a buddy growing up in Hoboken called Jimmy. Jimmy Left Nut, on account of the fact his left nut was way bigger than his right. Not sure why we knew that. He became a firefighter. I should call him, it's been wow, thirty, thirty-five years. Damn, I'm old. Maria, darling, can you take Jimmie here inside and get Betty to do what needs doing? He will replace Louie, that stupid idiot. Get him a shirt and get him started right away in the driving pool. Get him a cell phone and a pager, too. Kid, I might need you tonight for something. The best way to learn the job is to do it. Hey, director-man," he yelled. "Time to get this show on the road. I'm pumped up again, and I'm not paying these people to hang out on my lot. I got a business to run." He turned away without another word.

Maria gave him a smile. "Come on, follow me."

As they were walking into the dealership, Jimmie could hear behind him, "Action!"

"Look at these fucking beauties!"

"CUT!"

"Jesus Christ, what's fucking wrong now?"

"I'm needed out there," said Maria. "I'll hand you over to Betty here. Betty?"

"Yes?" Betty was an attractive woman with a short brown bob and tight flesh coloured shirt with a plunging neckline.

"My dad's hiring Jimmie here to replace Louie. Get him set up, please? Dad's up to his usual tricks on set."

"No problem. Jimmie, is it? Follow me, and we'll get you to fill out the paperwork."

"Thanks, Betty. And welcome to the Delvecchio family, Jimmie," Maria smiled. "As dysfunctional as it is." She headed back out to the lot.

He signed the papers he needed to do, and they gave him a beige button-up short-sleeve shirt with the logo for Delvecchio Chrysler-Jeep-Ram on its left breast. He pulled it on over his t-shirt. And he was off to work.

The work was simple enough. He drove a Dodge Journey wrapped as a moving ad for Delvecchio Chrysler-Jeep-Ram, with Big Sonny prominently on the hood, both sides and the rear of the van, his catchphrase 'Can You Believe It?' emblazoned underneath his image. Most people he drove didn't want to talk much, but a few engaged him in pleasant conversation. He returned to the dealership at 5:30 that evening, feeling the day had gone well.

In the lobby, a few salespeople and customers browsed the floor. The door to Big Sonny's office was closed, but heated voices from inside spilled out into the showroom. A narrow window ran parallel to the door, and he could see Sonny's hands wildly gesticulating.

"Hey Jimmie," said Betty, in the middle of turning off her computer. "Big Sonny asked me to tell you to wait for him. He wants to talk to you."

"Ok, thanks."

"The guys in the back have you set up with your cell phone and your pager. Here you go." She handed them over to him.

"Thanks again."

"My pleasure. Good night." As Betty left, he watched her long legs and curves walking away, her short tight skirt leaving nothing to the imagination.

Finding a seat in the lobby, he started going through the latest iPhone. He had never owned a smartphone; his old flip phone was enough for him until it broke, and they didn't have the money to replace it. He sat there, browsing the features and accessing the internet. This would change his lifestyle.

The furor in Big Sonny's office abated. Soon the door opened. A beautiful woman in her mid-40s came out. She wore a form-fitting red dress straining against her obviously enhanced bosom and a white sun hat with a matching red band on it. One hand held a white clutch purse; the other a shivering Pomeranian. She strode through the showroom without a glance at anyone and out the front doors. Sonny scowled behind her, watching her go with obvious distaste in his eyes.

"You wanted to see me, boss?"

"Yeah, kid, I did," said Sonny, distracted. "C'mon in."

Big Sonny's office was a love affair to New Jersey. A big poster showed the Jersey beaches. New Jersey licence plates hung on the wall, the state flag and photos of Big Sonny with such New Jersey luminaries as Jon Bon Jovi, Bruce Springsteen and the state's most recent governor. Prominent on his desk was a family shot: a much younger Sonny, a little girl Jimmie realized had to be Maria and a beautiful woman. The family in the photo beamed, their happiness evident.

The image differed from the scowling man hunched in his leather chair. The chair dwarfed the slight Sonny so much as to be comical. Sonny crossed his hands behind his head and put his feet up on the desk. "All right, kid, now that we're alone, let's go over what you're going to do for me. That woman is my wife, Sylvia. You and Sylvia stay as far away from each other as possible. Believe me, you'll be much happier for it.

"I got my start in Jersey, kid. I was a big deal up there. Started out as a grease monkey for a guy named Tommy Vigoda. Real prince of a man. I married his daughter, Sofia; may God rest her soul. She was a helluva woman. Gave me my precious Maria. Not a day goes by I don't miss her.

"My current wife, Sylvia, she's a Jersey girl with delusions of grandeur. She wanted to come down here. I'd have stayed put. But a man has needs, and when he's suffered a loss, he sometimes makes stupid decisions. So here I am. You're wondering why I'm telling you this, huh?"

146

"No, sir."

"I'm telling you this, so you don't think too badly of me and the things I'm going to ask you to do. My Sofia, God rest her soul, she was my queen, and I treated her as such. Never raised my voice with her, not once. Never strayed or had an eye for another woman. Why would I? I had a prime rib at home, and everyone else was Spam.

"But this one, she's bad news. I'd divorce her, but I'm not willing to give up half of what I have. So, we kinda coexist and avoid each other.

"But a man has needs. Me more so than most. I'm a goddamn sexual beast. That's where you come in. I gotta keep things on the down-low because if Sylvia ever found out, she'd ruin me. My old guy, Louie, he was discrete. Until they caught the idiot with drugs. You do drugs? I don't abide none of that shit around here."

"No, sir, I don't."

"Again, with the sirs. Stop it. I'm just Sonny. Listen, you keep your nose clean, be ready for me when I need you, and deliver friends of mine around from time to time. And anything else I may need from you, ok? You're my fixer, right? I need something done, I ask you to do it. Just don't draw attention to yourself."

"Ok, Sonny. But I have to ask, how am I supposed to drive around for you and not draw attention to myself when I'm in a vehicle with your face plastered on the side of it?"

Sonny stared at him blankly. "Holy shit. I never even thought of that. I've been playing goddamn Russian roulette all this time. You're already coming through for me. I got to get you a different car. Leave the damn Journey here; you want a Challenger?"

Jimmie perked up. "A Dodge Challenger? Sure!"

"Man, you're enthusiastic. I like that. But that brings me to tonight. I need you to pick up a friend of mine and bring her to me. There's a spot in Sarasota I will be at."

"Sarasota?"

"Yeah, Sarasota. You got a problem with that?"

"No. I've never been there."

"What? It's forty miles from here," said Sonny.

"Closer to thirty."

"And you've never gone?"

"Had no reason."

"You're weird, kid. But I can work with weird. Here's the address," he scrawled it on a slip of paper and handed it to Jimmie. "It's a little party for like-minded people. You need to bring Naomi up there for me tonight, ok?"

"Got it."

"She's getting her hair done right now. The salon's over by the Beall's store."

"I know the one you mean."

"Good man. I told her to look for the guy with the weird hair."

"Why does everyone call my hair weird? It's glorious."

Sonny looked at him and then broke out laughing. "Stop it, kid, you're killing me. Oh, God. You got an hour to go until you're to pick her up. Go get yourself something to eat; it will be a long night. I need you to wait around in Sarasota until the party's done so you can drive her home. These things end around 1:00. You won't have to be in until noon tomorrow, ok? Here." Sonny peeled off three twenty-dollar bills from a substantial bankroll he pulled out of his pocket. "I always get extra pumped up on filming days. I gotta blow off some steam. Go, go get something to eat. No booze, though; you can't be drinking on nights you are driving around for me, ok? Oh, and lose the shirt. You're right about not drawing attention to the lot."

Jimmie nodded and took off the beige Delvecchio shirt. "I think we understand one another. Let me get you the keys to the car. Naomi will appreciate it, too; she always hated that old Journey."

Sonny jumped up out of his chair, got him the keys from the sales desk and handed them to Jimmie. "Good luck, kid. You won't see me until tomorrow."

The car was easy to find. It was bright white and screamed 'awesome'. He got into it and sat there, enjoying the new car smell. He'd never driven a new car before, and never a car like this. Lovingly running his hands over the interior and gripping the steering wheel, he couldn't wait to take it for a spin.

But first, he had to call his mother. "Hello?"

"Hey mom, it's me. I wanted to tell you I got the job. I'm at work. Worked most of the day, and they've got me working late into the morning. I won't be home until well after midnight."

"That's good to hear. I'm worried about you. What's this job again?"

"I'm the personal assistant to Big Sonny Delvecchio, mom. The guy who owns those car dealerships."

"Is that the little man who is always yelling on TV? What's with you and guys who do their own TV commercials? He's not very professional and proper, not like Luther Monroe," she sniffed, sounding disappointed.

"Yeah, but Luther Monroe ended up not being very nice. This guy's cool, mom. I'll do ok here."

"Be safe. Don't do anything stupid."

"I won't, mom. Jeez."

"I love you, son."

"I love you too, mom." He hung up the phone. Wow, a cell phone and a sports car. This could end up better than the law office. *It's not as professional, I suppose*, he thought to himself. *And I'm not in a position to help anyone, but at least I'm appreciated. That's something, I guess.*

Jimmie hit the auto start button on the car, and the engine rumbled to life. The whole car shook with the power at his fingertips. He longed to take it out and test what it could do, but he had to show restraint. Getting a speeding ticket on his first day was not advisable. He had to show Big Sonny he was responsible.

Sixty dollars in his pocket meant no fast food for him tonight. He went to Checkers for a gourmet burger, onion rings and a drink. Then he went to find Naomi.

He walked into the salon. A stylist approached him. "Wow! What style! You look fabulous! Don't tell me you're here to lose that mane? A lion is less majestic without its mane."

Jimmie beamed. "Thank you. Not everyone recognizes the need to have a carefully cultivated style. But no, I'm here to pick up Naomi."

The stylist nodded. "She's getting finished. But Sugar," she said, looking appreciatively at his hair. "I would love an opportunity to play with that. We so often get the same boring requests. With you, I could create a real masterpiece."

Naomi came forward. Jimmie knew her at once. She was a younger version of Big Sonny's wife, Sylvia. Long, lean legs delicately balanced on ridiculously high heels, enhanced breasts, long nails, puffed up lips, and long brown hair squeezed into a tight, short blue dress intended to capture attention. She was Big Sonny's trophy and here to be polished before he displayed her to his friends. She paused when she saw him sitting there. "You must be the guy. Sonny mentioned you had weird hair. Let's go."

In a matter of moments, he'd had his hair put on a pedestal and then laid low. "My name's Jimmie," he said with a hint of coolness.

"I don't care. Can we go?"

He gestured towards the door and held it open for her; she strutted through it without a glance or a thank you. Her eyes scanned the parking lot. "Where's the stupid van?"

Jimmie gave her a smile. "No van tonight. We've upgraded." He pressed the door lock button on the key fob. The lights on the Challenger flashed. Naomi looked at the car. "You expect me to crawl in the back of that?"

"No, you can sit up front."

"With you?" she sneered. "Not a chauffeured ride if I sit in the front. Fine, it will have to do. Sonny and I will have a talk." She walked to the passenger door and stood there. "Well?"

Jimmie hustled over to the door and held it open for her. "Sorry," he said, indicating she should sit. She took his hand and used it to balance herself as she eased into the seat. He closed the door behind her.

It impressed her when he turned on the engine. Its power reverberated throughout the cabin. "Is there any music you listen to?"

"Are you trying to talk to me? Don't talk to me. The other guy knew better. You're the driver, not the talker. So, drive." She fished her cell phone out from her purse and took a few Instagram selfies of herself with various hair flips and duck face looks. He shrugged and headed out of the parking lot, leading to the highway north to Sarasota.

Naomi spent her entire time on her phone as they drove in absolute silence. Jimmie didn't even bother to turn on the radio, lest he disturb her, and would not engage her again. Instead, he concentrated on his driving.

He merged hesitantly onto the highway and stayed in the right lane. He kept it to five under the speed limit. Soon he got to the furthest north he'd ever been. This was a brand-new territory, in so many ways, for him. The highway sign declared Sarasota was twelve miles ahead. Everything was going smoothly.

They pulled off the highway and into Sarasota. The address ending up being a condo building by the waterfront. Tall, gleaming towers, taller than he had ever seen before, glowed with a strange luminescence in the fading light of the sun. Before long, they pulled into the parking lot of the condo. It had a doorman and concierge. *Fancy* thought Jimmie.

Jimmie put the car into park and opened the passenger door, holding out his hand to help Naomi out of the vehicle. She got out and smoothed her dress over her hips, and walked away without even acknowledging him. She didn't look at the doorman either as he opened the door.

"Are they always so rude?" he asked the doorman as Naomi disappeared into the elevator.

"Not all of them," said the doorman. "Those who earned their money, they aren't so bad. Most remember how they got here. They are used to dealing with different people. Those born into money, yeah, mostly they act this way. They've never had to work, or interact with anyone outside their own social circles, so they overlook us. But those trophy girls, they are the absolute worst. They start with nothing and have luxury handed to them. I can understand those born into it, not knowing how to act with people like us. These girls were us. But get a sugar daddy, and they get uppity."

"Yeah, I figured. This is why I never wanted to come to Sarasota. Too much uppitiness."

The doorman smiled. "The best thing about the trophy girls, though, is seeing them fall back to earth. They don't get kept long. Just long enough to get accustomed to the lifestyle. But it's not theirs. When the rug gets pulled out from under them, the crash is hard. I've watched some of them being dragged from the unit they lived in when daddy decided the girl to be no longer worth the hassle or they get a newer, younger model. Most bounce back with a lesser daddy. This life is fleeting, and they don't see the end coming."

This reminded him of Caroline. He wondered if she had been someone's trophy girl and was now relegated to hustling guys for drinks back at Gator's. It struck him as sad.

"Well," he asked the doorman. "I got a few hours to kill, and I don't know the area. Anything to do?"

"This place is mostly hoity-toity stuff. Beaches, shopping, botanical gardens, museums; I don't think that's what you want." He leaned in close and lowered his voice. "You looking for something a little...unseemly?"

"No. I'm on the clock. Nothing that will jeopardize the pickup. Thanks anyway."

"Goodnight, my man," the doorman said as he got into the car.

Jimmie picked up snacks at a gas station, picked out a paperback novel from a rack, found a well-lit park and read his book for a few hours. He returned at midnight.

At twelve forty-seven, he got a text from an unknown number. "You better be there," it said.

The elevator doors opened, and several people came out—mainly women; tall, leggy, curvy and young. Naomi wasn't with this group. The few guys with them were tall, straight-laced looking ex-jock types; security whose job it was to make sure the ladies made it out of the building for their

152

own safety and the discretion of others. Several cars in the parking lot started; people here to pick up their charges. The ladies and the men they entertained were not to be seen in public together.

The elevator opened again, and another group emerged. Naomi was with this group. She staggered and leaned on a pert, cute blond woman. Naomi appeared to wipe away a tear as she gave the woman a hug and then headed towards the door. Jimmie got out of the car. Naomi balanced on her heels with difficulty. She proceeded across the lobby and out of the door held open by the doorman. She had a dull glaze in her eyes as she paused and scanned the parking lot before her eyes alighted on him, and she shambled over.

He opened the door and held out his hand to help her into the car. She fell into it, her legs akimbo; he couldn't help but notice she didn't wear any underwear. She pulled herself into the car and buckled her seatbelt as he closed the door.

Naomi fell asleep. They were driving on the dark highway back towards Englewood when he realized he had no idea where to go. He'd have to wake her.

"Naomi? Miss? Excuse me, miss?" She didn't respond. He gave her a gentle nudge. She moaned and rolled away from him. Not knowing what to do, he pressed hard on the horn.

The sound jolted her awake, and she looked around, out of sorts and unsure of where she was. "What the hell?"

"Someone almost cut us off," he lied. "But now that you are awake, can you tell me where I'm taking you?"

"Oh," she said. She gave him an address somewhere in the Rotonda. She closed her eyes again and fell back to sleep.

Jimmie drove into the middle-class neighbourhood. The round winding streets of the subdivision (it looks like a spoked wheel on maps) were confusing, but he found where he needed to take her. It was a small, unassuming home, a newer black Dodge Ram pickup truck in the driveway (with a Delvecchio Chrysler-Jeep-Ram licence plate cover) and an older model Ford Focus. "I think we're here," he said, nudging her again.

"Hmmm? Oh." Naomi reached over and opened her own door before he got out of the car. She pulled herself out, rubbed her hands through her hair and straightened out her dress. For a moment, she looked less a trophy girl and more like someone playing dress-up.

Returning here to what he assumed was her parents' house was a reminder of her reality. She turned to him, acknowledging him for the first time since the salon. "Thanks," she said, giving him a wan smile. She turned and headed towards the door, fishing through her purse for her key. He waited until she found it, put it into the lock and disappeared into the house. The front porch light winked out.

Jimmie drove back to the trailer park. This job would be fascinating; it was an eye-opener. He realized unhappy people were going through the motions, and money and prestige don't make you happy. Part of it made him appreciate what he had with his mom and his friends. His life might not be perfect, but he had the things that mattered most. It was hard to believe only four days ago, he was off to his first day at the Monroe Group. It had been a hell of a week.

He entered his trailer, had a swig of soda and fell into his bed exhausted, wondering what tomorrow would bring.

Chapter 15

Stacy Keibler's thong was bright blue; he'd slept longer than intended. The night had taken its toll.

Jimmie strolled over to the bathroom and had a shower. He towelled himself off and took the chance of walking naked to his bedroom. Looking at his clothes, he thought: *I will need more than one Delvecchio shirt.* Yesterday had left it rumpled. He gave it a shake and hung it up to air out. *I should have hung it in the bathroom while I showered; the steam would have helped.* He had excellent ideas, but they often came too late.

Grabbing a fresh t-shirt and one of his remaining pairs of khakis he'd bought to work at Monroe, he had his cereal, beverage and smoke out on the patio.

He'd finished the cereal and was enjoying the nicotine haze when his mother wandered over. "Oh, why are you still here? I thought you said you got the job. Shouldn't you be at it?"

"I don't have to go in until noon, Mom. Hey, did you notice the car in the driveway?"

"I did. I was going to complain to Jerry."

"It's mine. Well, not exactly mine. They have furnished me with a vehicle to assist with my duties to Mr. Delvecchio."

"Be thankful you've got something. Although it made me proud when you said you wanted to study to be a paralegal. You did so well at that; I hope this job doesn't stop you from pursuing it."

"Mom, don't worry. I will. I like the perks. Big Sonny is more real to me than Luther Monroe in hindsight. I had delusions as to the person he is. I have no such delusions now. But," he stressed, "It's not something long term. It's not a career. It's a job, that's all it is."

Dolores sighed. "That's good to hear. I didn't want that terrible Mr. Monroe to destroy your dreams."

"He's a setback, Mom. Don't worry."

"I'm doing laundry. Any clothes you need washed?"

"In the hamper. Nothing is a priority right now."

"Ok." She kissed him on the top of his head and left to do the laundry.

He finished his cigarette and picked up his dishes. In the distance, he could hear the McCarthys. But seeing as he had gotten up later than usual, he'd missed the argument stage and came in at the make-up sex portion. He shuddered and went into the trailer.

He finished getting dressed and got in the car. It roared to life at his touch. He backed out of the parking spot and out into the path. He noticed Chester. "Wooeee, that's a sweet ride. Hey," said Chester. "You're not selling drugs, are you? A guy starts a new job, and he's got a sweet ride, one wonders what he's up to."

"No, Chester, I'm not selling drugs. I'm chauffeuring mistresses. It's slightly less unseemly and a lot less illegal."

Chester chuckled and gave him a wave. "Have a good one, my man."

Jimmie made it to the dealership before noon. He walked in and smiled at Betty. "Can I get some extra shirts?"

Betty nodded. "I'll order you another four; you can get them on Monday. Is that ok?"

"A-ok. Where's the boss?"

"Big Sonny has a VIP in seeing him today. Senator Phil Stevens is in his office. Sonny's a big supporter, a big fundraiser. When it comes election time, he'll loan you out and have you run errands for him."

"Oh." Phil Stevens, a Republican, had been Senator for the past eighteen years. Jimmie didn't have much use for him and wasn't looking forward to helping. This might be the motivation he needed to find a paralegal job elsewhere.

Big Sonny's door opened, and the Senator backed out of the office, shaking Sonny's hand while Sonny slapped him on the upper arm. They laughed, comfortable around one another. An aide to the Senator followed them out.

"Ah, Jimmie, c'mere. I want you to meet someone." Big Sonny waved him over when he saw him. "Jimmie, let me introduce a good friend of mine, Senator Phil Stevens."

"Hello, sir. I recognize you from your signs."

Senator Stevens reached out and took his hand in both of his in a vigorous shake. The Senator stood taller than him, a hair over six feet, his suit and tie perfect. He had manicured and moisturized hands and perfectly capped teeth. Even his breath was minty fresh. "Jimmie, nice to meet you. I always look forward to meeting constituents. And to support fine small businessmen such as Sonny Delvecchio here. Its men like him," the Senator releasing his left hand from the handshake to gesture towards Sonny. "It's men like him who are the true servants of Florida. They are creating great jobs for the people, and I am happy to play a part in helping make the conditions that allow him to thrive."

Sonny laughed. "You guys get that big tax reform bill over to the President to sign. That's how you'll help me the most."

Senator Stevens pointed his left index finger at Sonny. "Don't worry. The Majority Leader has been counting the votes, and we've got enough to pass it. It will be before the President to sign by Christmas, mark my words. And he'll sign it, as he promised."

"That's great news," said Sonny. "It'll help me. Now, can you get the President to lay off the social media?"

The Senator chuckled. "Sonny, if you can figure out how to make that happen, there'll be a Cabinet post for you."

The two men shared a hearty laugh. "Sonny, Jimmie, I have to go. I have a meeting later today in Naples with the Board of Trade. Come on, Jill," he said absently to his aide.

"See you, Jill." Sonny gave her a wink.

She looked familiar to Jimmie. Her blond hair pulled into a bun, and she wore glasses, but he still could not shake she was familiar to him. Then it hit him. She was the young woman Naomi hugged in the lobby last night. The Board of Trade meeting was not the only thing the Senator was in town for. Jimmie felt sick.

The Senator and his aide left, and Big Sonny came over and wrapped an arm around him. "Hey kid, you did good last night. Naomi made it home safe and sound. I'm pooched after being up so late last night; I'm going to make it an early night at home. You're off the clock tonight. Keep your pager and cell phone with you this weekend, though. I might need you for something."

Big Sonny looked uncomfortable. "I got to take back the Challenger. My baby, she wants to sit in the back. Don't worry, no soccer mom vans. I'll let you take a Chrysler 300 tonight. I mean, it's not super fancy, but they're nice. Betty'll get you the keys for the 300."

He started to walk back to his office and turned to glance back over his shoulder. "Check-in at the courtesy desk. They might need you to drive someone somewhere. You still work here." He entered his office and closed the door.

The rest of the day proved uneventful. Many had dropped their car off anticipating the weekend, so the dealership was hopping. They required all-hands-on-deck to handle the demand. He arrived back at the dealership before 6. He swapped out the keys for the Challenger for the keys to the 300. It was dark blue and still a sweet car. More luxurious than the Challenger, but it didn't have the gravitas.

On his way home, he called Rob on his cell phone. "Hey man, do you want me to pick you up at the marina?"

"You picking someone up for a change. Wow."

"Do you want a ride or not?"

"Yes, I do. Thanks."

He pulled into the parking lot at the marina ten minutes later. "That's a nice ride, ball sack. Who'd you blow to get that?"

"Ha, ha. Comes with the gig. But if you think this one's choice, you should have seen what I drove yesterday."

"What was it?"

"A Challenger."

"No way! Man, the SXT? Those are sweet." Rob got into the car.

"We going to Gator's tonight?" he asked as they headed to Rob's house.

"You got somewhere else to be?"

"Of course not. I'm making small talk. Ass."

"Hey, we were on the talk shows last night. Everyone cracked jokes about the alligator boys. I liked Kimmel's send-off on it," said Rob.

"If you're lucky, there might even be a sketch on Saturday Night Live."

"You think?" said Rob. "Wow, I always wanted to be on Saturday Night Live."

"Except you won't be on the show. It would be a character based on you but not you since they don't know who you are."

"Don't take this from me. I have so little going for me right now."

They pulled into the parking lot of the complex where the two brothers shared an apartment. "Since you have a car, be the DD tonight, give Ryan a break. He only ever gets to have two."

"What if he doesn't mind?"

Rob shrugged. "I'll ask him. But be prepared."

"Fine. But if I owe him, you'll be the designated driver for two years when you get your licence back. When is that, anyway?"

Rob scowled. "Another 13 months, Kemosabe. It's driving me crazy. There's no decent public transit around here."

"You'd take public transit?"

"No, the bus is for losers."

"You should get a bike."

"Bah. No way. Say hi to your mother for me." Rob got out, and Jimmie headed home.

Luckily Ryan said he was ok to drive. "Jimmie should be celebrating. It has been one heck of a week for him." Rob and Ryan swung by and picked him up around 8:30.

Gator's was extra busy tonight. Myrna barely had time to say hi and put their drinks in front of them. No booths or tables were available, so they went to the deck. Clint waited for them.

"Boys," he said as they came out. "Hey, I hear the boss likes you. He's got a special place in his heart for misfits."

"He must love you then," Jimmie said, causing his friends to laugh at Clint.

They found a less crowded corner, one where you couldn't see the alligators drifting sleepily below them. "Hey, you see us on the talk shows last night?" asked Clint.

"I liked Kimmel's the most. Which one did you guys like?" asked Rob.

"I didn't see any," said Ryan.

"Kimmel was fine, but I liked Seth Meyers," said Clint.

"Seth Meyers? He isn't funny."

"You like what you like, I'll like what I like, ok? Jimmie?"

"I didn't get to see any. Still, no TV, remember? I have to rectify that soon. And besides, I worked until after 1 a.m."

"What were you doing?" asked Rob.

"Driving around Big Sonny's mistress. Took her up to a weird sex party in Sarasota."

"Hey, our boy has popped his Sarasota cherry! Huzzah!" said Clint. Rob and Ryan huzzahed right back, and they took a drink.

"Ha, ha. It was a big gathering. Lots of girls getting dropped off. I think our Senator was there."

"Who?" asked Clint.

"Senator Phil Stevens."

"I don't know who that is. I'm not political."

"You don't know the Senator? Do you know who the governor is?"

Clint shook his head. "Nope. Don't care either."

"You at least know who is President?"

"Of course, dumbass. He's on the goddamn news all the time. You can't avoid him."

"I like him," said Rob. "Used to love his TV show."

"Ugh, he's terrible," said Jimmie. "He's a terrible human being. Don't tell me you voted for him?"

"No, I don't vote. Never do."

"What?"

"Me neither," said Clint.

"I'm surrounded by cretins. Come on, Ryan, at least don't make it three strikes."

"Yeah, I voted. I always do. It is important to vote. I voted Democrat this time. She was an accomplished lady and deserved to win," said Ryan. "I liked her."

"Oh please," scoffed Rob. "What's to like about that old shrew? She had a guy killed,"

"Use your head for something besides resting your cap on," said Jimmie. "She did not. Politicians make up stories about their opponents. They made up some whoppers about her. I can't believe how people fell for them."

"You can't tell me you like her? My idiot brother does. He never liked the President's show."

"No, I didn't like her. I didn't like either of them. I don't care if someone is a Republican or Democrat; I want good people in there. She didn't impress me, but at least she's not a total waste of skin like the President. I voted for her because she wasn't him. People voted for him because he

161

wasn't her. In a country with over three hundred and fifty million people, these were the best two for the job of President?"

"Oh, for the love of Christ," said Clint, rolling his eyes. "Enough with the politics. You say another goddamn word about politics, and I'm throwing the speaker over the railing to swim with the alligators."

"Ok. Politics always gets people riled up, turns friends and family against one another," said Jimmie.

"Damn, but since you mentioned it tonight, all I can think of is us being in a skit on SNL," said Rob.

"Wow. That's big-time," said Ryan.

"Hey, I never said it would happen. I said it could happen. They were already into rehearsals. It didn't blow up until Thursday, remember? Don't get your hopes up. And by next week, it will be old news, so they won't do it then."

"Yeah, well. A man can dream," sighed Rob. "In hindsight, it was funny."

"Nancy thought it was hilarious," said Clint.

Rob blanched. "Nancy? As in Nancy Monroe?"

"The same. How many Nancys do we know?"

"You told Monroe's WIFE we were the ones who threw the alligator into the doors of their family business?"

"Yeah. She had a good laugh over it."

"Jesus, Clint," said Ryan.

"I can't believe you did that. Have you met the mayor's wife? Or the sheriffs'? You sleeping with them too? Maybe tell them as well. They can all have a laugh."

"Cool your jets, pilgrim. What's she going to do? Tell her husband the guy she is sleeping with behind his back is the one who chucked the alligator through his door? C'mon, Jimmie's right. Use your head for something besides resting your cap on."

"Yeah? Well, maybe think with the right head, then, huh?" Rob hissed, trying to keep others from hearing them. "You know what, big man? This wasn't about Jimmie at all. You didn't give two shits about Jimmie. You roped us in to get back at her old man."

"Fuck you," said Clint, turning away.

"Listen, fellas, this isn't helping, ok? Calm down, Rob, he's right. She can't say anything without saying how she knows, and she can't do it without giving herself away. But Clint, damn man, you shouldn't have put us at risk like that," said Ryan. "They are talking about potential felony charges."

Clint sipped his beer and shrugged. "What's done is done. You can't change the past, no matter how much you want to. No sense wasting any energy on it."

"Whatever," said Rob. "You fucked us, man. I can't deal with you right now. I'm going inside. Leave me alone for the rest of the night, ok?" Rob left.

Jimmie couldn't help but think Rob was right about Clint's motivations. Clint was the mastermind. He pulled the plan together quick; maybe he had been thinking about it in the back of his mind. He would never have gotten them to help but for Jimmie's firing. Clint saw an opportunity, and he took it. Wasn't that what he'd said to him Wednesday night?

The argument put a damper on things. It was hard going back and forth between Rob and Clint. Rob grew morose as the evening went on until Ryan pulled the plug before eleven and said he was going home. Rob would have argued about cutting it off so early, but he was happy to get out of there. They dropped him off at the road, and he walked into the trailer park from there.

The park lay still. The cool night air held a touch of humidity. It was clear out, and he could see the stars above him blazing away on the dark backdrop of the sky. He lit a cigarette and strolled around the perimeter, taking his time getting back to his own trailer. When he got there, he mounted the steps, butted out the cigarette in his ashtray on the patio table, and went inside. What a week this had been.

Troy Young

Chapter 16

Jimmie's phone and pager were silent all weekend. Big Sonny had found something else to preoccupy his time and left him alone. He took his mom out in the big 300 to run errands. The comfort and smoothness of the car impressed her. "Don't get into trouble," she said to Jimmie. "He's crude."

Jimmie couldn't deny Big Sonny had a vein of crudeness to him. "He's not the most couth person I know, that's for sure. He has elements to him that are questionable. He said no drugs, so that's something in his favour. And he'll have my back as long as I have his. It's a symbiotic relationship."

"Make sure the relationship doesn't become parasitic," said Dolores. "You get out if he takes advantage of you."

Later after the errands, he took the car out on his own. It had been so long since he'd had access to a car, and he enjoyed the freedom. He rolled down the windows and turned up the music to make sure everyone heard and saw the man with the sweet hair in the luxury car.

Once over the bridge towards Englewood Beach, he made the right-hand turn at the roundabout. On his right, patrons on the front patio of a bar stared across the road towards the beach. Still a few hours from the sunset, but the outdoor front patio was busy. As he glanced at the terrace, his eyes alighted on her. Caroline. He slowed and drifted by, trying not to look at her but still observing her out of his peripheral vision. She looked up, and he saw her looking at him. She had to recognize him with his distinctive style. She saw him driving this luxury car. *Too bad I didn't still have the Challenger. She'd be impressed.*

He drove north, past the beach and then past a series of vacation rental units. He turned around before he got too far and started into the area with private homes. How long should he wait until he drove back past the bar? On his drive back, the driver's window would be closer to her so she'd get a better view, and he might give her a nod or a smile or a wave or something. He needed to time this right. Pulling over to the side of the road, he sat and agonized. Too fast, and he's stalky. Linger too long, and she may have left or moved inside the bar.

After what seemed half an hour of debating (but was only seven minutes), he started the car. He drove towards the roundabout as slow as possible without being obvious. The bar came into sight. His heart dropped; she wasn't there. But no one else occupied her seat, so maybe she hadn't left? He drove past the bar and back into the roundabout. He considered going around the roundabout and heading back the way he came to try again. But as he got ready to exit, she came out of the bar. Jimmie panicked. She had to spot him in the roundabout. Instead of exiting, he continued to drive. He was now on his second pass. She watched him driving in circles. The guy in the seat next to her said something to her, pointing at the car. She snickered, still looking at him. This left no choice but to continue and exit at his first opportunity. This took him away from the beach. He gunned his engine as he fled the roundabout; the big V8 Hemi roared, drawing attention to him as he sped away. "Smooth Jimmie, smooth," he said to himself, embarrassed.

#

When he awoke on Monday morning, the skies were dark. A severe storm rocked Englewood. The palm tree next to the trailer lashed its fronds against the steel walls. No lounging for him on the deck this morning. The storm altered Jimmie's changed routine, disrupting his ritual. No sun on his face this morning would ruin his day. An ill omen indeed.

He arrived at the lot and noticed the storm had blown the inflatable men off their moorings, and the gorilla flapped and pulled at its tethers. The mood inside the dealership proved as dark as the outdoors. Salespeople milled around, as no one shopped for a car in the middle of a small hurricane. Big Sonny was in a foul mood. Jimmie heard him speaking with Betty when he entered. "... those cocksuckers won't come and tie the damn thing down. They say it's too goddamn dangerous. It's going to damage my roof and land on the cars."

He spied Jimmie. "There you are," he yelled. "Listen, kid, I need you to do something. Get on the roof and secure that stupid gorilla. My people here forgot to deflate it last night. The guys who installed it are being big pussies. They don't want to get wet."

"Me? Up on the roof? I know nothing about strapping down an inflatable gorilla."

"Jesus Christ, it's not goddamn rocket science. Go figure a way to secure the damn thing."

"This sounds dangerous."

"Life's dangerous, kid. It was dangerous to get out of bed this morning. It was dangerous to get behind the wheel of the car you drove here. You might have choked eating breakfast. We face danger every goddamn day."

"I'm not sure I can."

"Listen, kid, I hired you to be my fixer. So, fix it, all right?"

"Can't one of the guys from the shop do it?"

"What?" said Big Sonny. "One of my shop guys? They are too valuable. And the salespeople," he gave them a withering glare. "The salespeople are too useless. Look, kid, I have faith in you. I know you can do this. I trust in you to do this." He put an arm on Jimmie's shoulder and looked him in the eye. He lowered his voice. "I thought I had found something special in you, kid. I sure hope I don't need to find myself a new fixer guy."

He either climbed out on the roof or handed over his keys. The third day on the job, like Monroe. No way was he going out the same way. "You got a ladder?"

"Thatta boy. Nah, no need for a ladder. There is a set of stairs that go up to the maintenance hatch. Listen, 5 minutes tops out in that weather. And hey, I'll give you the day off, with pay. The other drivers can cover; people have been cancelling their appointments today." Sonny looked around. "Someone give Jimmie a raincoat!"

One lady in the billing department loaned him her coat, bright pink with white hearts.

"What the hell are you wearing?" Clint laughed at him, entering the shop. Clint wore his work coveralls, his hands covered with grease, a Dodge Ram pickup suspended on the lift above him.

"It's called a raincoat. Big Sonny wants me to go up on the roof and strap down that big gorilla."

"Need help?"

"No, you big monkey. I can't lose a trained mechanic," said Sonny, coming into the back. "Your boy can handle it." Sonny wore a black raincoat. "Kid, I'll be outside on the ground shouting out instructions to you. You might not see what I can see." He slapped him on the back. "Teamwork, son."

"Is it still teamwork if I'm on the roof, and you're on the ground?"

"Hey, generals stay in the back and direct the foot soldiers. I'm a general, and you're the soldier. Soldier on, boy."

Jimmie found the narrow steel stairs leading to the roof. They climbed to a narrow gangway and then a ladder to the hatch. "That's it," said Big Sonny, giving him two thumbs up. He climbed the ladder up to the hatch and unlatched the handle holding the door tight to the roof. As the hatch started to rise, the wind took it and slammed it violently open. Driving rain lashed him from the now open hatchway, pouring into the floor.

"Careful kid, careful," said Big Sonny, looking at him anxiously. Clint stared up at him, absentmindedly rubbing his hands with a rag.

Jimmie climbed up the last few steps into the storm. The wind and rain buffeted him. His hair plastered to him as the rain drove in under the hood of the raincoat. Water trickled underneath it against his skin. The hearts on the raincoat were changing colour as they got wet. It created a surreal moment for him, holding on to the hatch, watching the colours change.

The sounds of the straps holding the gorilla being whipped by the wind broke the spell. He looked up at the gorilla. It hung above him like a cyclopean monster out of another age, thrashing in the wind. They had turned the blower off, so it was no longer inflated, but it performed a macabre dance above him. The straps and their metal clips were being pulled tautly and whipping back on themselves.

"You up there, kid?" shouted Big Sonny. Even with his bellowing voice, he could barely hear Sonny over the wind. He made his way closer to the edge. Sonny stood on the lot below, so Jimmie gave him a thumbs up.

"Should we try to pull it in? I could try to grab it and roll it up and shove it into the hatch. The gorilla is acting like a sail; no gorilla, and there's nothing to pull the straps."

"You do what you think is best. I'm not on the roof," yelled Big Sonny.

"No, you are not," he whispered to himself. "I shouldn't be. Why didn't they deflate the stupid thing and bring it in last night before the storm hit?" He shrugged his shoulders and shook his head. Why was he the only one thinking?

He made his way back to the gorilla, trying to grab the fabric, but the wind pulled it out of his hands. He'd have to jump on it and use his body weight to hold it. He leapt, landing in the middle of the fabric pile and hit the roof, hard. Because the fabric was so expansive, the wind threatened to roll him off the balloon. He started to scramble on the gorilla, trying to bunch up the loose fabric into a large ball beneath him. A twenty-foot-high inflatable gorilla had a lot of material.

He got most of the soaking wet cloth bundled up underneath him. The straps lay on the ground. Jimmie struggled to pull the sodden mass as he stood, fighting his way towards the closed hatch.

Arriving at the hatch, he wished he hadn't closed it, as he needed to open the door while holding on to the gorilla. The strap furthest from the hatch strained against the wind. He'd need to unhook it along with the other straps. He could hear Big Sonny yelling below, but he couldn't make out what he said, and he wasn't going to let go of the balled-up balloon to go find out.

It was a challenge to keep it in place under him and get to the strap. The strap pulled so tight he couldn't release it. He needed to move back at least a foot to give him the slack he needed. Fighting the buffets, he got the strap loose. The second strap proved easier. It had slack, and he'd learned how they worked while struggling with the first one. He released the second strap.

Strap three took no time. The ball of fabric under him became dishevelled as he worked on the straps. Only one left. He tried to pull the fabric in close.

At that moment, a massive gust of wind grabbed at the loose fabric and bucked Jimmie off of it. The wind took hold of the gorilla, causing it to unfurl and blow high into the air. No longer held by three of the four tethers, it billowed out like a misshapen kite connected to the roof by a single yellow fabric strap.

The balloon whipped itself side to side in the strong wind. He grabbed hold of the strap attaching it to the roof. He pulled on it until another massive gust took hold and lifted him up off the roof. He clung on and then let go, dropping three feet to the roof.

The (Extra)ordinary Life of Jimmie Mayfield

Jimmie landed hard, his left leg buckled beneath him, forcing him to one knee. He looked up at the gorilla above him, looming there, a creature ready to squash him like a bug.

And then it happened so fast. He heard a loud ping, and then a sharp pain developed in his lower right jaw as he lifted off the roof. Then falling, followed by blackness.

#

Jimmie started to become aware of the intense pain in his jaw. Then he realized he felt dry, and no wind, no rain lashed him. A heavy warm blanket pressed him onto the bed; he heard strange buzzing and whirring sounds.

Opening his eyes, the sudden light stabbed into them and caused him to swoon. He felt nauseous. Closing them against the light, in the moment they were open, he had seen the white tile ceiling above him, fluorescent lights illuminating the room—a hospital. Groaning to himself, he worried how much this would cost.

He heard a man's distant voice, loud and frantic. The words were unintelligible at first, but as awareness returned, he could tell what they were saying.

"...doc, do whatever you can for him, ok? I told him not to go out on that roof, but the kid, he idolizes me. Thought I'd be proud of him or something. I said, 'Kid, don't you go out there. We can fix a roof, we can write off a car if need be, but we can't replace you.' And he did it anyway, doc, he did it anyway. You got to help him; he's like a son to me, you see? Whatever it takes, I'll pay for it. I'll pay for it. I'll cover his costs. Put him in a private room, spare no expense, all right? Just make him better."

"Well," said another voice, a female. "He has a broken jaw and has suffered a concussion. Lucky for him, he landed in that palm tree, or this could have been worse. He got a few minor bumps and cuts, but if he had hit the concrete, he'd be dead."

"Oh, no," wailed Big Sonny. "But he will be ok, doc?"

"Head injuries are tricky. He's been unconscious forty-five minutes, which gives me concern. We didn't see any bleeding in his brain, so that's good news. He might have memory problems, confusion, mood swings, etc. If he's lucky, he only ends up with a dreadful headache. We'll know more when he wakes."

"Thanks, doc. Please do whatever you can. Remember, I'm taking care of everything, ok? Everything."

Silence hung for a few moments. Jimmie tried to turn, but the pain was excruciating. He gave a slight groan and settled back.

"Kid? Kid, you awake?" Big Sonny loomed over him, near his face. "You ok, kid? Want me to call the doc?"

He nodded weakly and tried to give Sonny a thumbs up.

"Ok, you lay there, kid, and take it easy. Get well. Don't worry about anything, ok? I'll cover this, all of it. Get you the best care money can buy." Sonny's mouth rested by his ear. "If anyone asks, you went up on the roof on your own accord, ok? I got a whole bunch of people back at the dealership who know otherwise, but they won't ask them if you go along with this, ok? Don't think about suing me or nothing; you won't get anything. You try that, and I'll have you killed, all right? I know a guy. You'll fucking ruin me, and I will not let that happen, ok? You understand me, and I'll take care of this. I can be your friend or your enemy. You don't want me as your enemy. So, let me be your friend. We friends?"

"Friends," Jimmie groaned out through his wired-shut jaw.

"All right, kid, all right. I got your back. On everything. Friends." Big Sonny stood. "And for what it's worth, kid, I'm sorry. I shouldn't have made you go on the roof. I went too far. It won't happen again." Sonny's voice receded. "Doc? Hey, doc? He's awake. He's awake."

Chapter 17

Jimmie avoided any serious injuries. The concussion proved not severe. He had headaches and nausea, but the other symptoms were minor. The broken jaw was an inconvenience. He had a stable fracture, so no need for surgery. But his mouth needed to be wired shut for the next four to six weeks. That was a bummer. Tomorrow night was Halloween, itself of no consequence to him, but that meant Thanksgiving was only four weeks away. Eating pureed turkey and mashed potatoes through a straw wasn't appealing.

One of the most significant casualties of this accident, though, were his mutton chops. When the errant strap with its metal end hit him and broke his jaw, it tore a large gash in his face. They stitched the wound, and the doctors said the scarring would be minimal. They had to shave his glorious facial hair. They salvaged the moustache, but Jimmie lost the large sideburn part. "Shave the other side," he told them. Feeling like Sampson after Delilah had cut his hair, he resigned himself to make do with a moustache.

Clint lingered at the hospital; he and Big Sonny had followed the ambulance. Clint insisted on being able to stay, and Big Sonny relented. Clint sat in the big chair beside Jimmie's bed.

"Man, that was messed up. You shouldn't have been up there. Or I should've helped you."

"It's OK," he said through his clenched teeth. "He was frantic and not thinking straight. If he thought something might happen, he wouldn't have forced me onto the roof. Although he said if I tried to sue him, he'd have me killed, that he had a guy."

"Big Sonny? He's a paper gangster. He talks tough, he acts tough, he claims to be connected, but he's a big wuss, a real softy. Sonny doesn't have a guy, and he couldn't go through with it even if he did. You got nothing to worry about. You should sue."

"If he takes care of my medical bills as he said, keeps paying me while I'm off and lets me keep my job, it's ok. I can't catch a break, and I'm not going to lose another job. What would I get, millions? Lawyers will take half. I'll be making a dickhead like Luther Monroe richer. Besides, money like that is dangerous. I did nothing while poor; imagine how much nothing I'd be doing while rich? Getting an award would be detrimental to my personal development."

"You can be one weird dude sometimes. If that guy doesn't come through with his promises, though, buddy, he'll answer to me. I got your back."

"Thanks, man."

Jimmie spent two days under observation at the hospital. True to his word, they housed him in a private room with round-the-clock care. Upon his release from the hospital, Big Sonny drove him home himself.

""Listen, kid, I'm glad you're doing ok. I got a few surprises for you at your house. But first I need you to sign some papers, all right? This one says you in no way hold me or my companies responsible for what happened to you, and you waive any right to a settlement. This one is for the Department of Labor since the accident occurred at work. It's an affidavit that I told you to stay off the roof. Despite my warning, you put yourself in a dangerous situation by going out there in the storm. I will face a fine either way," Big Sonny shrugged. "But, this will limit the fine and allow us to keep operating."

Sonny held out a pen. Without reading the papers, Jimmie signed them both. "Excellent, kid. Wait until you see your surprises at home."

Big Sonny attempted to buy his loyalty, concerned about what this could do to the business. He'd replaced the trailer's air conditioner with a working one. In the living room sat a fifty-five-inch television, complete with the best cable package offered. A PS4 and a variety of games were found beside it. "I figured you'd be laid up for a while, so I got you a few things to help keep you occupied." In Jimmie's room was an adjustable bed like the hospital, to aid in his sleeping and recovery. "Best mattress on the market. And that thread count on the sheets; you'll never get out of bed." There was a TV in there too.

Dolores beamed at his being home. She'd warmed to Sonny. She had heard Sonny's version, and Jimmie had no reason to fill her in on the truth.

"Listen, kid, I got to get back to the lot. Take all the time you need to get better, ok? Your job will be there for you when you do. I will keep paying you, too, the entire time you're off. I know a good kid like you will want to rush back as soon as he's able, right?"

Jimmie nodded. "Attaboy. Dolores, you take care of our boy here."

"You got it, Sonny. As soon as he is up and ready, I'll send him right back to you. And thanks again for the air conditioner."

"My pleasure," and he left.

#

As the concussion symptoms were still lingering, he couldn't take advantage of Sonny's gifts right away. When he tried to watch TV, he ended up nauseous and got a headache. The first week, he slept. The bed, he had to admit, was excellent.

In the second week of his recovery, he started to feel better, but because he wasn't eating much on account of his jaw, he lost weight and had low energy. But he could watch TV and even tried out a few games for an hour.

His friends stayed away most of the first week to let him rest, but starting the second week, they started stopping in one at a time to see how he was doing. Myrna even stopped by one day unannounced. There came a knock at the door.

Myrna stood on the patio, nervously glancing around the park. "Oh, hey," she said, smiling when he came to the patio door. Jimmie stood there, shocked for a moment, staring at her. "What are you doing here?" he said.

His lacklustre greeting caught Myrna off-guard, but she recovered. "Well, my favourite customer hasn't been around, so I thought I'd come to see you. Rob told me what happened, how your boss sent you up onto the roof in the storm and how you got hurt, but you were recovering at home. I thought I'd come by and say hi." She stood there for a few moments. "Are you going to invite me in?"

"What? Oh, yeah, sure. Where are my manners? My mother would be so disappointed in me." He slid open the door, and Myrna entered. Her eyes took in the trailer's entirety with its shag carpeting and its knickknacks. He glanced around and grew embarrassed at his shabby little sanctuary. The television which dominated the room offset this. Still, given how this had been his convalescent retreat for the past couple of weeks, his little nest of blankets and dirty dishes had added a level of funk to the general mustiness of the trailer.

If she noticed, Myrna gave no sign. Her being here was awkward; he did not want her to witness how he lived.

"This place brings back memories," Myrna said, her smile returning. "The place I grew up in, I swear we had the same carpet."

"Yeah, but I still have it forty years later, while you ripped it up a long time ago."

"It might be still there. I moved around a lot when I was a kid. It was just my mom and me after my dad ran out on us."

"I'm sorry to hear that."

176

"Why? I was three. It was a long time ago. Still, this trailer brings back memories. It's a time capsule."

"I've thought that. There is this story of a woman who had to flee Paris at the start of World War II. She closed her apartment and left the city. She never returned to it. Nobody entered her apartment until she died seventy years later. The place was frozen in time. Our trailer is like that, but instead of priceless works of art, we have this stuff. Most of the stuff is my mom's. I'd never have chosen this," he picked up an ugly little statue of a man with the saying 'I'm down to my last nerve, and you're on it!' printed at the bottom.

"Or this," said Myrna, picking up a porcelain cat with the words 'Are you kitten me?' painted on it.

"That one's mine."

"Oh, I'm sorry," Myrna said, blushing, putting it down hastily.

"I'm kidding. It's not."

"Ass." Myrna playfully slapped him. Her eyes alighted on the couch. "Ohmigod, is that a Snuggie?"

"It is. Again, my mom bought it, but dammit, it is pretty cool."

"I've always wanted to try one out! Can I?"

"Mi casa es su casa. Go ahead."

Myrna picked up the flowered throw from the couch and put her arms in the sleeves. "How do I look?"

"Fetching.".

"It's a comfortable set up you have here. And look at the size of the TV!" she said, sitting on the couch and pulling her legs up under her, covered by the Snuggie.

"Big Sonny gave it to me because he felt guilty. Before that, we had nothing." He shifted uncomfortably.

"I think it's fine. You should see the place my sister and I share. It's cramped. This trailer is bigger than it, and you have a patio and outside space. You've got me beat."

"Thanks," he said, struggling to comprehend how this dilapidated old trailer would be an upgrade for someone. "So, you have a sister?" He realized he didn't know much about Myrna outside the context of the bar.

"Half-sister actually. My dad's a deadbeat who found a series of women with low self-esteem to take him in and put up with his bullshit for a time before he moved on," she said, unimpressed. "Margo is one of the few offspring I know about. I'm sure there are some I'm not aware of. Still, she's cool. We get along ok, but I'm more her surrogate mom than her sister; she's still in high school. Her real mom is a hot mess, so I've had to step in to make sure she has a chance."

"Wow."

At that moment, Dolores interrupted their visit. "Jimmie, I wanted to check on you. How are you... Oh!" Dolores noticed Myrna, sitting on the couch covered in her Snuggie. "I didn't realize you had a friend over," she said, casting a sideways glance at him, a sly look on her face.

"Mom, this is my friend Myrna," he blushed. "She works at Gator's. She stopped by to check on me."

Myrna jumped up. "Hello." Realizing she still wore the Snuggie, she pulled it off, embarrassed.

"I'm pleased to meet you, dear. Sit, make yourself comfortable. I can see my boy is in good hands," she said with a twinkle in her eye. Jimmie wished the spongy floor would give way and suck him into the centre of the earth.

"I stopped by because I thought he might want company," said Myrna.

"My poor boy hasn't been able to go anywhere, and it's been hard on him," said Dolores coming over to ruffle his hair; he started to wish the fall had killed him. "But he's a good boy, genius and caring, and he's good to his mother. He's quite a catch."

"Oh, god, mom."

"I don't want to interrupt what... whatever you were doing. Three's a crowd. It's nice to meet you."

"It's nice to meet you too, um Mom?" Myrna said.

"Dolores, dear. But you can call me Mom if you'd like."

"Out!" he said, wanting to die.

Dolores gave him a kiss on the cheek. "She's nice," she whispered.

"She's very nice, yes," he hissed to her. "Now get out of here."

"My boy needs space without his mom. I get it," she winked. "Go easy, dear; you're still recovering."

Jimmie steered his mother to the door and didn't push her out but made it clear it was time for her to go. Dolores smiled at him and gave the two of them a wave through the glass before she left. He watched his mother leave before he turned back to Myrna, who smiled at him. "She's cute," Myrna said.

"Yeah, cute."

"Oh, come on, she is. She cares about you. And parents are supposed to embarrass us; you'll embarrass your kids someday too. Better to embarrass them like she did, then to be a constant source of embarrassment like my father," she said as she sat back on the couch.

"I guess," he said, a hint of coolness in his voice.

Myrna's smile faded. "Maybe I should go?"

"What? No, don't. I'm thrilled you're here. I'm… I'm worried about what kind of host I'm being. Please forgive me; I'm still off from the injury. Please stay, don't make me beg. It'll be unbecoming, but I will if you make me."

Myrna's smile returned to its full glory and lifted his dark mood. "I might want to see you beg," she said coyly. "But since you're still recovering, I'll take a rain check. Should we watch a movie or something?"

"I'd like that. Can I offer you something? I don't have snacks, but I can get you a drink. Do you want a Diet Coke?"

"You know what? I think it's time we turned the tables. You should bring me a beer for a change, and I can sit back and enjoy it while you wait on me?" she laughed. "If you have any, that is."

Jimmie prayed he had a beer in the fridge, and he wasn't a religious man. He opened it hesitantly; lucky for him, someone had stuck a six-pack of Yuengling in there. Whichever of his friends had done so, he silently thanked them. "Glass, or is the bottle ok?"

"I'm not fancy. The bottle will do."

179

He poured himself a Diet Coke and brought Myrna the
bottle of beer. "I can't drink beer on my medication."
"This truly is a role-reversal then."
He chuckled and turned on the TV.

Chapter 18

By the time week three of his recovery rolled around, Jimmie was up playing video games. His headaches and concussion symptoms had abated. He started to get hungry, and this made him grumpy. By the end of the week, he was going stir crazy.

His friends asked him if he was ready to go out to Gator's. "I'm not supposed to drink on my pain medication," he informed them. "They prescribed oxycodone to me, but I was so worried I'd become addicted to it or someone would find out I had it and break into the trailer; I mean, my mom's stash of medicinal marijuana freaks me out, but add oxy to the mix, and I might as well cook meth in here because I'd be living every trailer park drug house fantasy. They switched me to Tylenol 3s, but you can't drink when using them. It's too hard on the liver."

"You can go to a bar and not drink," said Ryan.

"Pfft. As if," said Rob.

"I'd love to get something to eat, but everything is still being sucked through a straw."

They took him to McDonalds (not that McDonalds), and he got himself a triple-thick strawberry shake. "A Friday night, and I'm at a McDonalds sober," bitched Rob. "I haven't done this since I was 14."

"And doesn't that put your life into perspective for you, hmmm?" said Ryan.

"Shut up."

By the fourth week, Jimmie started to venture out on small errands. He took his car to the mall and picked up a big tub of protein powder. Jimmie began making fruit smoothies with the powder and started feeling energetic. *Why didn't I do this sooner?* he thought. Again, great ideas, often late.

On Wednesday, the day before Thanksgiving, he had a doctor's appointment. He hoped for good news; Thanksgiving was the culinary high point of his year, and he'd hate to miss out.

He got checked by the doctor. "Mr. Mayfield, everything has progressed well. It is time for us to unwire your jaw. Just in time for Thanksgiving," she said.

"Doc, I could kiss you.".

"Please don't. I don't want to call security."

"Right."

Sonny called him later that night. He'd been checking in every few days. "So kid, how'd it go today?"

"I got unwired, so I'm pumped."

"Hey, that's awesome to hear. To celebrate your fortune, I got a surprise coming your way, ok?"

"What is it?"

"It wouldn't be a surprise if I told you. Just wait, OK?"

"Ok."

"We got a great Black Friday sale on this weekend," Sonny boasted. "I always hold a soiree Saturday night at the lot. We close at 5:00 and get it gussied up for a private event, invitation-only, for my best customers—great deals only for them. I move a ton of product at this thing. If you're up to it, I'd like you to be there."

"Wow, thanks."

"You can drive, right?"

"Yeah."

"The guests may need a drive home if they've had too much to drink."

"Oh," he said crestfallen. "I'm not a guest?"

"Kid, are you one of my best customers? C'mon, man!"

He headed over to Chester's trailer on Thanksgiving. It surprised him to see his mom wasn't making dinner. "I didn't think you'd be able to eat, so I bought nothing to make for Thanksgiving. Besides, that's such a big undertaking, and I'm not up to it anymore. Sorry baby."

"Don't worry, I order in Chinese food. You like sweet and sour chicken balls?" Chester asked him.

It crushed Jimmie. All he hoped was his jaw would be unwired before Thanksgiving, and he'd be able to enjoy a traditional feast. Sweet and sour chicken balls were not an adequate substitute for turkey and mashed potatoes and gravy and stuffing and...

Throwing himself on the couch, he resigned himself for what was sure to be the worst Thanksgiving ever. Chester sat in his recliner, watching football. "Man, I love Thanksgiving," said Chester. "Nothing goes together like Chinese food and football. You watch football?"

"No," he sulked.

"Too bad, because there's a lot of football here today."

He contemplated going back to his trailer and drowning his Thanksgiving sorrows with a couple hours of video games. Killing zombies was more festive in his mind than Chinese food and football. There came a knock on the door.

"I wonder who that could be?" said Dolores with an exaggerated expression of surprise.

He grew wary. Something was afoot.

Dolores opened the door. Three people were standing on the front porch, large insulated bags of food in their hands. The graphic on their jackets' breast and painted on the van visible over their shoulders said Bon Appétit Catering. "Is this the Mayfield party?" the man at the door asked.

"Yes," answered Dolores.

"Your Thanksgiving feast is here, courtesy of Sonny Delvecchio."

"Come in," said Dolores.

The three people unpacked the food and laid it on the counter. Everything you needed for a Thanksgiving feast came out of the bags. There was a turnip casserole, garlic mashed potatoes, gravy, a whole turkey (which they carved), cranberries (sauce and jelly) stuffing, and a fresh pumpkin pie. "Oh, and we had an added ask," the man said, opening up a container of sweet and sour chicken balls. "Oh, man," said Chester, "now we can celebrate Thanksgiving."

"Mom, you knew about this?"

"Of course, dear. Did you think I'd let you miss Thanksgiving? What kind of mother do you think I am?"

"A crappy one, I thought."

"I told Sonny how much you love Thanksgiving and how you were nervous you wouldn't enjoy it. He told me he'd take care of everything. If you still couldn't eat solid food, we'd have turkey soup," Dolores said. "I'm so glad we're not."

Jimmie was in bliss. After a month of eating liquid, he wanted to gorge himself on solid food. For it to be the traditional Thanksgiving feast, well, he felt euphoric. His mom was an adequate cook, her Thanksgiving fare passable, but he liked it so much he didn't care. But, this year's repast proved superior to anything she'd ever made, nay, that he'd ever eaten, that at this moment further Thanksgiving meals were ruined. But he'd worry about that next year. For now, a drumstick had his name on it.

#

On Saturday, he cleaned himself up for the event at the dealership. Sonny had asked him what size suit he wore. Jimmie had never owned a suit, so Sonny sent someone over to measure him. They later returned with a simple black suit and a black tie. He looked like a guy from Reservoir Dogs in it. *I could get used to this style,* he thought.

He combed out his horseshoe moustache. It had grown on him, so much so he hadn't bothered to grow the chops back. He tried something new with his hair. He pulled his mullet back and secured it with a ribbon. Now he looked less

Jean-Claude Van Damme in Hard Target and more Steven Seagal in Above the Law. That, the suit and the moustache made him feel damn good.

He arrived at the lot before any of Sonny's guests.

"Wow, kid, look at you! You are looking good. That suit makes you look like a gangster," said Sonny, coming over and giving him a hug. Sonny looked at his face. "You can barely see that scar. Too bad. It would have made you a badass. We knew this guy back home, Paulie Ciccarelli; he had this big scar he got when someone busted a beer bottle in his face. We called him Scarface after that, you see? Man, the ladies loved that scar. Paulie really made out with the broads."

Jimmie had no comeback for that. He nodded.

"Kid, hang back, out of the way. Let the caterers do their thing. I don't want you drinking nothing on account of how I need you to drive. But help yourself to the hors d'oeuvres. Just don't make a pig out of yourself, all right? Don't talk to no one either; leave that to the salespeople. I need you close by. This is a big deal for us, the biggest day of our year. I'm counting on ya."

"Can do, boss."

"That's the spirit, boy."

The courtesy drivers were out front, acting as valet parkers for Sonny's guests as they arrived. The sales staff greeted them at the door. Everyone dressed up for the occasion; men in suits, women in gowns. It was one of the main events in the Englewood social calendar.

Jimmie found it funny to watch these well-dressed people getting drunk as the evening progressed. Their cultivated personas started to devolve as they consumed alcohol. He realized no matter how successful someone might be or stuck up they were, get a few drinks in them, and they weren't much different from the clientele he encountered at Gator's. They were better dressed, and he admitted, smelled better too.

A ruckus started near the front doors. A female voice grew high-pitched, almost a yell.

"...you tell that little rat Sonny to get over here," the shrill voice cut the air, drawing him over to the doors.

"Miss, you have to go," said one of the sales guys.

"Don't touch me! I want to see Big Sonny. Big Sonny, ha! More like Little Rat Sonny. Little Rat Sonny Delvecchio. He can't get rid of me that easily."

He recognized Naomi. Her hair dishevelled, and her make-up smeared. She was intoxicated. Sonny came running.

"Naomi! Get the hell out of here! You're causing a scene!"

"Sonny. Oh, Sonny." She reached out towards him, trying to embrace him.

He grabbed her wrists. "You got to get out of here. Now!"

"How could you do this to me, Sonny? How? Did I do something wrong? Baby...please..."

Jimmie should do something. He was Sonny's fixer, right? Besides, Naomi knew him. "Can I help?"

Sonny's eyes went wide. "Kid, get her out of here! You do this, and you're saving my life. Whatever you want, if I can give it, you got it. I want her gone before my wife hears!"

Jimmie reached over and took Naomi's arm. "Naomi, we need to go. Please." He nodded to one of the sales guys. He opened the door. Another one of the sales guys took hold of her other arm, and before she could react, they both rushed her through the door.

"Stop it! You assholes. Sonny! Sonny!" she began to kick and thrash. "Help!" she yelled. "Rape!" Lucky for Sonny, the door had shut, and her last words were drowned out by the music. Only those closest heard the disturbance.

Outside Naomi kicked and fought, trying to get back into the dealership. "Look, if you don't settle down, we will call the police. You are trespassing at a private function," said the sales guy holding her arm.

"No need to call the police. She will come with me. I will take her for a drive, get her to calm down." Jimmie looked right into Naomi's eyes. "Please, let me take you home."

"It's over," she sobbed. "Sonny dumped me."

"Oh, sorry. You think this will win him back?"

"No. I want to hurt Sonny. Like he hurt me. All he cares about is his stupid cars, his reputation. And he's so scared of his wife. I wanted to watch him squirm." She looked back at the front doors and yelled, "Sonny! You son of a bitch! Agggh!" She began to kick again.

"That's it, I'm calling the police," said the sales guy, fishing out his cell phone. "I'm not paid to be a bouncer."

"No, I'll take her. Naomi, you don't want to be arrested on top of this, do you?"

"No," she whimpered.

"Then let's get in the car. I can take you anywhere you want to go, ok? You can't stay here."

She wiped a tear from her eye, looked back towards the doors and spit at them. "Screw him. Let's go."

He steered her towards his car. The sales guy opened the passenger door, and they guided her inside. She sat there, staring straight ahead.

"Good luck with that one, buddy," said the sales guy. "You'll need it." He headed back into the dealership.

Jimmie got in the car. "Where do you want to go?"

"I don't care," she said. "Just drive. Away from here."

He started up the car and took a left out of the dealership, deciding to head towards Punta Gorda. Not because Punta Gorda was special, but it was in the opposite direction from Sarasota.

They drove in silence for half an hour. Naomi started to shake her head. "That bastard," she spit. "The things he had me do. I knew he would not leave his wife. He's too chicken shit for that. I'd at least expected he'd set me up in a condo or something. Give me one of those cars."

"You were using him? To get something out of him?"

"Oh, don't be so goddamn naïve. It's the way of the world. Guys like Sonny Delvecchio want a pretty face on their arm, and they will throw money around to get it. He gets his eye candy, and we get looked after."

"Not... respectable, is it?"

She shook her head. "Who gives a shit about respectable? What, you want me to go get a job at some bar, shilling drinks so some guy can grab my ass for tips? Would that be respectable? Go work at some minimum wage job? I guess it would be respectable, but I'd be poor as shit."

"So, you were willing to...prostitute yourself, so you didn't have to work at a shitty job?"

"That's an ugly word. I'm not out giving hand jobs in alleys for ten bucks. I'm not a whore," she sniffed. "I'm a mistress," she tried to say with dignity. "A kept woman. History is filled with them. No one called them prostitutes."

They drove in silence. Soon they crossed the elevated highway, which leads into the north part of Punta Gorda.

"I should turn around and take you home."

"How do you know where I live?"

"I took you home once. To the Rotonda. After... Sarasota. The party with the Senator; I saw you hug his assistant in the lobby."

"Oh," she blanched. "That night. Fuck. Sonny's such an asshole." Naomi started to dig into her purse and pulled out a small flask. She opened up the top and took a swig. "You want a swig?"

"No, thanks. I'm driving. Open alcohol near the driver is illegal. Please put that away."

"Whatever." She took one last swig and put it away. "Want to do coke?"

"Only coke I do is of the diet variety," he said.

She laughed. "You're funny. You know that? I mean, you look funny, but you are funny too."

"Thanks...I guess."

"You sure you don't want any coke? I could let you do it off my tits?" she said, pulling open her neckline, exposing the top of her breast. "Or do you prefer it off my ass?" She undid her seat belt and got on to her knees, her back to him, pulling up her skirt, exposing her thong. She looked at him over her shoulder and bit her lip.

"Put your seat belt on, please. It's not safe to drive without your belt on."

"You're such a prude," she said, laughing. She sat back into her seat but did not put her seat belt back on. She leaned closer, her breath hot on his neck. "I hate that little bastard, the way he used me—things he had me do to his little old body. And for nothing. I want to get back at him. You want to help me get back at him?"

"I have no reason to get back at Mr. Delvecchio. He looks after me."

"I want to get back at him. Help me get back at him." She stuck her tongue in his ear. He swerved on the road before he brought the vehicle back into his lane. "What the hell are you doing? You trying to get us killed?"

She laughed at him and sat back in her seat. "You want a blow job? I could suck the chrome off of a motorcycle tailpipe."

"Don't see how that's supposed to be sexy or appealing," he said, keeping his eyes dead ahead.

"I'll let you fuck me. You can even put it in my ass. You can do me anywhere you want."

The decision to head towards Punta Gorda came back to haunt him. Why had he not stayed near the Rotonda?

"Come on, I know you want it. It'll be unlike anything you ever had." She spread open her legs, pulled her thong aside, exposing herself.

"It's not going to happen. I'm taking you home," he said, looking straight ahead, unwilling to glance at her.

"Oh, why not? I'll bet you're hard. Let me check." She lunged forward and grabbed his crotch through his pants.

"Whoa! Stop it. I told you it's not going to happen."

"You fucking loser! You are such a goddamn loser! Freak! I hate you!" She threw herself back into her seat and put her head in her hands. She started to cry. "I can't even get a loser to fuck me now."

He continued driving, not knowing what to do or say. An attempt to console her would be mistaken for interest. A thought jumped into his head. "I'm gay."

Naomi sniffed and looked over at him. "What?"

"I said I'm gay."

"Oh," she blurted out, stunned. "Gay?"

"Yep. So very gay."

"Oh," she said again, starting to laugh. "Oh, I'm sorry. It makes sense now. I should have guessed, with that moustache.

"I'm sorry. I shouldn't have come on to you. I want to get back at that little shit." Naomi sounded introspective. "I wanted to be a dental hygienist. Or maybe a real estate agent. I don't know. There isn't much here to do in this town. I was still trying to figure out who I wanted to be when I met Sonny. I had gone with my dad to pick up his truck. Sonny charmed me; he made me laugh. And he's rich. I mean, he's old," she shuddered. "But when his guy slipped me a note saying Sonny wanted to take me out to dinner, it overwhelmed me. He wined and dined me. Took me places I'd driven by but could never afford to visit. He took me to parties, where I met many rich people, but always discrete. We needed to keep it quiet so his wife wouldn't find out. He started buying me things, bought me these," she squeezed her breasts. "Anything I wanted, he'd give it to me, except for a house. By now, I'd met the girls who the rich guys brought to these events. They told me what they were getting from their guys. I guess I fell into it. God," she gave a sob. "What have I done? What have I become? I am a whore."

"You were young and impressionable, and a rich guy showered attention and gifts on you. I think it's easy to get caught up in it. You found yourself swept up in things. I don't think you should be so hard on yourself."

"Thanks," she said, looking at her hands. She realized she wasn't belted in, so she put her seat belt back on and straightened out her clothes. "I still feel like such a fool. I let him use me."

"You did. But it's over. You won't do it again. You can't change the past. A friend of mine once told me regret is a wasted emotion. It changes nothing. What's done is done. But," he looked over at her. "It doesn't have to define you going forward. You can't change it, but don't let it drag you down, like an anchor. Don't let it stop you from going

190

forward. Going forward is not a straight line. You can go side to side and still be moving forward."

"Wow." She sat there, looking at him. Her mascara had run, and her lipstick had rubbed off. "That's deep. Are all you gays deep guys?"

"I can't speak for all gay guys; I can only speak for me."

That got a laugh out of her. "Do I have my first gay friend? I've always wanted a gay friend."

"I don't think so. I'll always be a reminder of Sonny and where you were. Go find a gay friend who can help take you forward." He hoped she bought it; in his own head, it sounded idiotic.

"Yeah. I need to put this behind me. But I'm keeping the tits."

"Obviously."

The entrance to the Rotonda appeared before them. She'd be home in 5 minutes, and he'd be free. This was one hell of a night.

"I don't even know your name?" she said as they pulled up to her house, not remembering it from the time he drove her.

"I'm James," he said, not want to give her his real name. "James Warr...ing..ton? James Warrington."

"Well, James Warrington, thank you. I was such an ass tonight."

"That's anchor talk. You're going forward, remember?"

She smiled again. "You're too smart to be driving for that asshole."

"Goodnight, Naomi."

"Goodnight, James." She leaned in and gave him a quick kiss on the cheek. She got out of the car and entered her house without a glance back.

Jimmie let out a deep sigh when the door closed. He needed a cigarette and a Diet Coke.

There were three left in his pack and no soda on him, so he stopped at a gas station. He pulled into the station and parked in a spot near the store.

"Evening," nodded the guy behind the counter as he entered. "Good night?"

"Weird night. A very weird night, man."

"Hey, we've all had them. I hear you, brother."

He grabbed two bottles, placed them on the counter and took out his cash. "Pack of Pall Malls, too, please."

"Sure thing," the cashier said, sliding the pack towards him. "Hey, you want to buy a ticket? Draw's on Monday."

"Ticket? For what?"

"Mega Millions. It's up to over five hundred million dollars, man. Imagine what you could do with that."

"The lottery is for suckers. Your odds are astronomical. We'd have a better chance of a panther coming through the door right now and eating us both."

"Still, man, someone has to win it. And think of all that scratch."

"That kind of cash will ruin someone. Be careful what you wish for."

"So two sodas and a pack of Pall Malls. Anything else?"

Jimmie was about to say no but glanced at the flashing Mega Millions sign. It was a sucker's bet, but someone had to win it. And if you were smart, you could avoid the pitfalls of a big win. Most people weren't smart. "You know what? Throw in one of those tickets. What the hell?"

"What the hell indeed, buddy." The cashier added a ticket to the purchase. "Good luck."

"I've had lots of luck, but not much of it good lately. It's about time something positive happened to me." Jimmie left.

Chapter 19

His cell phone rang at eight thirty-six, waking him. He saw it was Sonny calling and answered. "Hello?"

"Hey, kid. Tell me, what happened?"

"I got her in the car and took her for a ride. When she calmed down, I took her home," he said, yawning. "She won't bother you again."

"Why? Did she say that?"

"She's done with you."

"Well, that's a relief."

He shouldn't say anything, but what Sonny had done didn't sit right with him. "You treated her poorly."

"Poorly? What do you mean, poorly?" an agitated Sonny replied. "I wined and dined her at the best places. She did things she never would otherwise. Naomi knew the deal. If she didn't want it, why did she go for it, huh? Why'd she stay? Why is she so upset I ended it?"

"I guess that's part of what I meant, you ending it."

"Kid, I caught her doing coke. I told you, the one thing I don't abide by is drugs, right?"

"Yeah, you did."

"That was a deal-breaker. Naomi knew it going in. The lifestyle got to her head. She couldn't handle it. I don't see this as my fault."

"She expected a house out of you."

Big Sonny laughed. "Yeah, don't they all? I might have got her one, someday. What she didn't tell you is when you set up a mistress in a house, it's because you've picked up another side piece. You set up a safe house, and you go there to see them because you're now wining and dining someone new."

"What? That's messed up."

"The world's fucked up, kid. I don't make the rules; I live by them. Listen, kid, thank you for taking care of her for me. There's a little extra for you at the lot tomorrow. Enjoy the rest of your day." The phone clicked dead.

The next day he drove to the dealership. Betty had his shirts, something he'd forgotten with the accident. An envelope waited for him. He tore it open and inside found ten, crisp, hundred-dollar bills; Sonny had given him a thousand dollars. This gig proved to be more lucrative than he imagined. So much so he realized he hadn't thought about getting another paralegal job. Granted, he'd been recovering, but still.

His first day back proved dull; he drove people back and forth as required. He never ran into Sonny, and they made no requests of him outside his regular mundane tasks.

That night he picked up Rob and Ryan and drove them to Gator's. Rob's assertion that Jimmie should pick up the slack from Ryan as a designated driver had stuck with him, and it was time to reciprocate. Besides, he didn't want to drink much tonight.

Rob was already buzzed when he got to the brothers' apartment. He wore a t-shirt which read *'Two girls short of a threesome.'* "Boys," he said. "I got a feeling I'm getting lucky tonight." Ryan looked at Jimmie and rolled his eyes behind Rob's back.

When they got to the bar, Jimmie ordered three beers for them. "Glad you're back," Myrna said to him, handing over the beers. "I missed seeing you. Yours is on me."

He hadn't seen her since her visit to the trailer. Her visit had been a high point of his convalescence; they had spent the evening talking and watching two movies. It had been a delightful evening. "Thanks, Myrna. And thank you for visiting me at home. It was sweet."

She gave him a warm smile. "It was nice. I hope we can do it again."

"You get an awful lot of free beer from her," said Ryan when he showed up with the beer.

"C'mon," said Rob. "You haven't seen it? She's sweet on our boy. The way she looks at him, smiles at him, gets extra mad at him when he says something stupid or gets goo-goo eyed over Caroline." He took a big swig of his beer. "I'm going to mingle. You two will cramp my style. Never going to get laid sitting around here with you guys." Rob disappeared into the small crowd.

Ryan watched him go, shaking his head. "He's in a dark place. He's getting unhinged and gets angry quickly. I don't know what's gotten into him. I'm getting worried."

"What is it?"

Ryan shrugged. "I'm not sure. Hey, you never told me what Claire said a few months ago when we ran into her here."

"She said she still loved Rob. What she hated was Englewood. She felt trapped here. She'd hoped Rob would go after her."

"That explains one thing, at least."

"What's that?"

"A few weeks ago, after your accident, Rob took the bus up to Jacksonville. He didn't say why, but I suspected it was because of Claire. You should ask him about it."

"I will." He was curious about what Rob had done, what was bothering him.

"He's been so obsessed about getting with someone else," said Ryan. "Scary obsessed. But it's weird. You know how Clint goes on about women? The way he talks *about* women is not the way he talks *to* women, right?"

"Right. I mean, I'm sure his success rate would drop if Clint talked like that to women. I don't get to see him in action often, but I'm sure."

"Yeah, well, my brother isn't. He's convinced this is the secret to Clint's success, and this is how he should approach it."

"You're kidding."

"No, I'm not. That stupid t-shirt he's wearing? He says it's an ice breaker," said Ryan, shaking his head. "I had to talk him out of wearing one that said: '*Cool Story Babe, Now Make Me A Sandwich*'."

"That's pathetic. I mean, we're pathetic, but even for us, that's pathetic."

"Yeah, well, he says at least he's had a relationship with a woman, so he knows better than me."

"Just because you haven't dated anyone doesn't mean you don't get to state your opinion. I mean, I've never had a serious relationship either."

"Yeah, but I've never been with a woman. I mean, never."

"What? No way. I'd know this, wouldn't I?"

"Why? Not something I broadcast. I mean, I've made out with a few girls in the past, but that's it. I want my first time to be with someone special. Not saving myself for marriage special, but not with a random person. I haven't met anyone."

"Why didn't I know this? As your friend, I should have known this."

"It's no big deal. It doesn't bother me. I'm not hard done by. Where am I supposed to meet someone? After a person graduates from school, there aren't many chances to meet people. Sure, there's my work, but the women are in their 50s or older, or if they are younger, they've got a dude. The only women I interact with are the seniors who come into bowl or the moms bringing their kids. And this place," he said, gesturing. "It's not where I expect to meet someone special. At least not for me."

"You sound too picky."

"Picky?"

"Yeah, picky."

"Do you like our options here?"

"No."

"I don't see anyone expressing any interest in either of us here or anywhere."

"Hey, speak for yourself. Saturday, I had a hot woman offer me the chance to snort coke off her ass, and then she exposed herself to me."

"What!?" said Ryan. Jimmie filled him in on what happened on Saturday. "Man, that's messed up. And you didn't go for it."

"Nope. Didn't seem right."

"Well, I'm impressed with your self-control. Can't imagine my brother turning down that offer."

"Meh. He'd surprise you. Many guys would go for it, but I'd like to think we're better than that."

"Even Clint?"

"Yeah, even Clint. Clint even more. He gets offers everywhere, unlike us. Speaking of Clint, you guys seen him much?"

"Not since he told us he told Nancy Monroe what he did. Rob's still pissed at him."

"That's not good. We must smooth things over there. But you still sound picky to me."

"What I want isn't at Gator's." Ryan took a drink of his beer. "I haven't met the right person. I mean, I hope to settle down, get married and have kids. But some days, I feel I'm in a holding pattern. That we're all in a holding pattern."

Jimmie had to admit it was true; they seemed to be in this pattern. He'd lamented his own lot in life, but he never thought of his friends. He figured they were happy where they were. "What about what Rob said? About Myrna having a thing for me?"

"I don't know. Maybe?"

"That helps a lot, thanks."

"Sorry. I'm not observant to the cues women give off. Do you like her?"

"I dunno. I never thought of her like that. She came to visit me while I recovered. And when I got fired, I wanted to talk to her. Maybe there is something there."

"So, ask her out."

"No."

"Why not?"

"Say she says no? This place becomes awkward for us. I wouldn't want to ruin what we have here."

"What we have here? You looked at this place? That sounds like someone who likes the rut he's in. It's an excuse. Or you're holding out for Caroline."

"What? No way." It sounded unconvincing.

"Yeah, you get weird when she's around. I don't get it."

"She's hot."

"It doesn't matter how hot she is. If it hasn't happened, why will it?"

"Maybe I thought someday I would be able to offer the life she'd want. I can't do that living in my mother's trailer now, can I?"

"Ah, ha. You admit you've been holding out for her then."

"What? No, that's...shut up." He looked away and took a drink of his beer.

Rob came back into the room. He followed a short, cute woman. Rob tried to engage her in conversation, but her disinterest in him was obvious even from where they sat. "If I pick you up, does your friend come with you?" She whirled on him and threw her drink in his face. "Leave me alone, you creep!"

"Wait," Rob sputtered. "It's a joke. Because of my t-shirt. See?"

"And this passes as humour for you?" She grabbed a drink out of her friend's hand and threw it into Rob's face too. "Go save your brother."

"Come over here, Cyrano and sit," said Ryan taking Rob by the arm. "Keep Jimmie company. I'm going to walk around." He left.

Rob grabbed a napkin and mopped up his face. "Bitches be crazy."

"For a start, don't refer to women as 'bitches', and maybe you'll get somewhere. Did you think that would impress her?"

"I don't know, man. How does Clint do it? He gets more women than he can handle."

"Do you want to be like Clint?"

"Damn straight, I do."

"Really?"

"No, not really. It's just, I don't know...dammit." Rob put his head in his hands.

"Ryan told me you went up to Jacksonville. You acting like this, is it related to Claire?"

"He told you, did he? Figured he would. I know you want to ask. Nothing to tell; nothing happened."

He sat and stared at him. Rob started to shuffle in his seat. "What? Ok, fine, but I need a refill before I go down that rabbit hole with you." He ordered another beer. "Ask away."

"So, you went to Jacksonville. You went after Claire?"

"Yeah. You told me she'd hoped I'd go after her. I haven't shaken that since you told me. I wondered if the statute of limitations had passed. Ryan drove me to the bus station in Sarasota. Took the Greyhound. You can drive there in four and a half hours from here; the bus took eight—eight long hours. What made sense before I got on the bus didn't make sense after five hours on it. She left me. She said she wanted me to follow, but that's messed up. She could've told me how she felt."

"She said she didn't want to make you choose."

"Choose? There was no choice, man. I would have walked away from this," he gestured around, "in a heartbeat for her. She was everything to me."

"She said you wouldn't want to leave your family, your friends, your dream job."

"Sorry, partner, hate to burst your bubble, but I could. For her, I could have done anything." He shook his head. "What hurts the most is she didn't think I would. I thought she knew me better."

"I don't know what to say."

199

"Yeah, well, that's why I got on that bus. But then I started thinking of how I acted when I saw her last, and that by now she must have moved on. Didn't want to show up and see her with a new guy and for her to shoot me down a second time. I couldn't handle it. When the bus got there, I sat in a bar across the street from the bus station. Sat there for two hours, trying to find my courage to go to her. But I never found it. I bought a ticket on the next bus home." Rob sagged. "I'm such a loser."

"You're not a loser."

"Yeah, I kind of am. We all are. I will be thirty next year, the same as you. When we were in high school, is this what you imagined our lives would be at thirty?"

"I expected more than this, I suppose."

"I'm single, fat and nearly bald. I work as a gas jockey at a goddamn marina." He shook his head. "After high school, when I got my job, I was on top of the world. I loved the boats. They paid me to hang out with boats. I thought I had arrived. But I want my own boat, not working for assholes who own them. I will never get to that point doing this. This is why I was so hard on you for not having a job. You are the smartest guy I ever met, and thought you'd do something big. But you are lazy as shit, man. I work my ass off at a menial job, getting nowhere, but what else can I do? You could do so much and aren't doing a damn thing, and it pissed me off. And it pisses me off that Clint is the most successful of us. Don't even get me started on Ryan. Play Bowl! might as well be his tomb."

"I had no idea. I feel like a bad friend now."

"Bah. We're not women. We don't sit around, pouring our hearts out over tea and cookies."

"And just like that, Rob is back."

"Fuck off. Men don't do feelings and shit. We bottle it up and get drunk."

"That's old school toxic masculinity right there."

"Reading your mom's magazines again?"

"Now it's my turn to tell you to fuck off."

Rob laughed. "We're a fine bunch, huh?"

"Yeah."

"I'm starting to understand what Claire meant about Englewood. I didn't at first, but..."

"Englewood is fine. The grass is always greener somewhere else, right? Plenty have built the life they wanted right here. If not, your marina wouldn't be filled with those fancy boats, would it? Sonny Delvecchio has done well for himself. A person can make it right here. We each have our own path, and for some, staying here is it. For others, their path takes them elsewhere."

"This from the man who has barely left the county."

"I always thought this was the place for me. I'm comfortable here. But..."

"Yeah," said Rob. "But."

"Well, this has turned out to be a great first night out for me in a month. First, I find out Ryan's a virgin, and then this thing with you bringing me down."

"You didn't know Ryan is a virgin?"

"Not the kind of thing that comes up often in casual conversation, is it?"

"I guess not."

"Hey, what did you mean earlier about Myrna?"

"She's clearly into you."

"Why do you say that?"

"Exactly what I said earlier. The way she looks at you, the free drinks, and how you piss her off. A man only pisses a woman off like that if the woman cares. If she didn't, nothing you said or did would get a rise out of her. Look at the guys she has to deal with around here, all the crap. I don't see her getting mad at them like she does with you."

"I hadn't noticed."

"You should go for it."

"That's not a good idea."

"It's an idea. There's no way of knowing if it's good or bad until you ask. You got other prospects?"

Jimmie thought about what Ryan said earlier about Caroline. "No."

"We should decide we will do things differently. Again, tick-tock, thirty is coming. Worst case scenario, she says no, and you are right where you are right now. I made a mistake not going after Claire. Don't you make a mistake by not taking a shot at Myrna. You got a job now, you're making money, what's holding you back?"

"You're right. What have I got to lose?" He drained his remaining beer. "All right, here goes. Wish me luck."

Jimmie stood up and took a deep breath. Before he could change his mind, he strode up to the bar.

"Hey," Myrna smiled. "Another beer?"

"Nah, I'm good. I got to drive," He stood there nodding his head.

"Ok. You want anything else?"

"Nope."

Myrna looked at him. "Ok, then. I need to serve my other customers." She turned and started to walk away.

"I wanted to ask if you'd like to get a coffee, or ice cream or dinner or something? I'm not sure what we'd do, but something?"

"Jimmie Mayfield, are you asking me out on a date?"

"I think I am."

"You think you are?"

"Nope. I am. Yes. I'm asking you out on a date."

"I have a strict 'no dating of the customers' rule..."

"Oh, I guess that makes sense. Um..."

"I guess," Myrna smiled at him, "you must drink somewhere else then."

"But I enjoy drinking here."

"I guess in this case I will need to make an exception."

"Wait, does this mean you're saying yes?"

"Yes. I'd love to go on a date with you."

"Ok, then. How's this weekend?"

"Well, I work Saturday, but I'm free on Sunday if you want to do something."

"Yes, I do. Sunday."

"Call me later this week, or I'm sure you'll be in here before the weekend, and we can talk then."

"You bet." Jimmie turned around to face Rob and gave him a thumbs-up, and Rob returned it. "We should leave," he

202

said to Rob when he got back to the table. "Before anything screws this up."

"Let's go. The best chance I had was with the girl who threw the drink in my face, and I don't think that's working for me."

The two shared a laugh and looked for Ryan.

Troy Young

Chapter 20

A full coloured Stacy Keibler greeted him the next morning. His convalescence had messed up his routine, and he hadn't settled back into his previous one.

When he showed up at the dealership, excitement hung palpably in the air. "What's up, Betty?"

"You haven't heard? Somebody in Englewood won the Mega Millions last night. Fred in Parts organizes a ticket-buying pool for the office. He's not in yet, and we haven't been able to reach him on his phone. Everyone's excited we might have won." She leaned in and added, "A few are worried we won, and the reason he's not here yet is Fred's gone to collect the prize himself and skip town. You can't trust anyone when this much money is involved."

He had forgotten the ticket he purchased Saturday night. "You know the odds of winning? I wouldn't count on it."

Betty looked at him. "And what are those odds when you have found out someone local has won it?"

"Yeah, I guess that increases them astronomically," he admitted. Suddenly the ticket made his wallet heavy. He resisted the urge to pull it out right there and check.

The doors to the dealership hissed open, and Fred entered. Everyone looked up with anticipation. "You guys are excited to see me. Why I wonder?"

"Oh, spit it out. Did we win or what?" Betty said.

"Oh, yeah. That little draw someone in town won. I think you should sit..."

"Really?" Betty squealed.

"No, not us. Sorry folks, but we got to keep showing up to work."

The air sucked out of the showroom. For those brief few hours this morning, everyone had been planning in their heads how they would spend their winnings. Their dreams disappeared in an instant as the stark reality hit.

For Jimmie, the opposite occurred. With his coworkers' tickets taken out of the equation, his odds increased, at least a small amount. It was surprising how quickly he changed from thinking it was a sucker's bet that brought more problems than good to wondering if he might be the winner.

He went to the bathroom and entered a stall. With shaking hands, he pulled his ticket out of his wallet. Then he took out his phone and Googled the winning numbers. The top link was to an article on how the winning ticket was purchased in Englewood, Florida. The report said there was only one winning ticket. He scrolled down to the numbers. He looked at his ticket.

The numbers matched. An exact match.

The End of Book One

Chapter 1:
Lifestyles of the Rich and Jimmie Mayfield

Holy shit. Jimmie Mayfield's knees grew weak, and his head swam. His phone slipped from his hand, and he reached for it with the hand that held the winning ticket. Five hundred and twelve million dollars. The ticket slipped from his grasp as he missed the phone. Instead, it flew and hit the stall wall and fell to the floor. The ticket fluttered and bounced off the rim of the toilet. Instead of falling into the toilet, it landed on the floor beside his phone. He picked up both of them.

Jimmie kissed the ticket. Then the sudden realization the ticket had touched both the toilet's rim and the men's room floor hit him. But he didn't care. He folded it and stowed it back in his wallet.

His mind raced. What was he going to do? *I have to get out of here.* He needed to go somewhere neutral, somewhere safe where he could be alone to think. He remembered his thought from the other night. If you were smart, you could avoid the pitfalls that came with such a big win. *I need to be intelligent.* He needed a plan.

He left the confines of the bathroom. "Betty, I'm ill. I think it's a leftover from my concussion. Tell Big Sonny I came in but couldn't stay."

"Are you ok to drive in this condition?"

"Yeah. I'll be fine. I need to go home and rest."

"You poor thing. I hope you feel better."

"Thanks," he said, heading out the door and crossing the lot to his car.

He drove home and ran into the trailer. On his phone, he Googled 'what to do if you win the lottery.' A Forbes article came up, and he scanned it. He read he should sign the back of the ticket. He ran over to the junk drawer, the same junk drawer that inhabits every kitchen, and rifled through it. He couldn't find a pen. He was sure he'd find a pen. The drawer held a bunch of useless stuff, like a crusted over tube of Crazy Glue, twist ties for garbage bags, a pair of scissors, a Scotch Tape dispenser (he scratched his knuckles on the cutting surface as he dug through the drawer's contents). It was filled to the brim with old take-out menus (some places he noticed weren't even in business anymore, but he still didn't remove them from the drawer).

He sucked on the faint drops of blood that rose on his scratched knuckles. Frantically he started looking around the living room. Apart from an old plate from two days ago and a few empty glasses, there was nothing of interest. He began to pull up the couch cushions. He found a button, seventy-four cents worth of change, two hairpins and an old pen under them. He wanted to check to see if it worked before he marked up the ticket. He went back to the junk drawer and grabbed the menu on top. Gripping the pen, he drew circles on the menu. It left nothing but gouges in the thick paper. He threw the pen in disgust.

Then he remembered that his mother liked to do the crosswords in her supermarket magazines before her eyesight started to fail. *There might be a few pens on her bedside table.* He paused outside her door. It was open a crack. He didn't want to enter her room. It was an invasion of her privacy, and he was leery about what he might find.

Lucky for him, from the doorway, he could see two pens sitting on top of a small stack of magazines on her bedside table. Making sure he didn't look around the room, he strode to the table, grabbed them, and ran back out.

He searched around the kitchen table. *Where was the ticket?* His heart raced, and he scanned the floor under the table. Then he realized it was still in his wallet. *I need to relax,* he thought. He took a few deep breaths and willed himself to calm down. He poured a large glass of Diet Coke and forced himself to sip it. Then he took out a cigarette and lit it. *Mom will have to understand,* he thought. Then he took the ticket out of his wallet, smoothed it flat on the table and signed his name where indicated on the back. It was now officially his ticket. He breathed a sigh of relief.

He looked back at the article. 'Remain anonymous,' it said, 'if your state allows it.' A Google search told him Florida did not allow it. *Ah well,* he thought. *What's the fun of being anonymous?*

'See a tax pro' was the next thing it said. Jimmie needed to decide if it made sense to take the whole five hundred million paid out in instalments over the next thirty years or whether he should take a lump sum. Instalments gave him over sixteen and a half million a year, before taxes. *Lump-sum,* he said to himself. 'Avoid sudden lifestyle changes' was number three on the list. He looked around at the decaying trailer. "Yeah, right," he laughed.

'Pay off your debts.' He had none. 'Assemble a team of legal and financial advisors.' Hmmm, ok, he'd do that. He glanced at the others on the list. 'Invest prudently' 'Live within a budget' 'Take steps to protect assets' 'Plan charitable gifts' and 'Review your estate plan.' Apart from protecting his assets, the rest was boring. *Isn't that why I need a legal team?* That had to be his first step. He only knew one lawyer in town, and there was no way the Monroe Group would benefit from his wealth. Not after firing him.

He opened a new window on the phone's browser and looked up lawyers around Englewood. This gave him thirty different ones from which to choose. He eliminated those from the list that had no reviews or less than four stars. This left him with eight. Seven, he corrected himself, as the Monroe Group was one of the eight that fit his criteria. He hit the number in the first listing, and his cell phone began the call.

"Bialystock, Brooks and Schwartz," a pleasant woman's voice answered. "How may I direct your call?"

"Yes, I'd like to speak to one of the named partners, please."

"Please hold." After a brief wait, he heard. "Leo Brooks."

"Mr. Brooks, I've come into a large amount of money, and I need legal representation to help with protecting my assets and long-term planning."

"Well, we'd be happy to help you. I can set up an appointment for say, tomorrow morning at ten-fifteen?"

"I could make it then. But first, one question. What is your opinion of Luther Monroe and the Monroe Group?"

"Mr. Monroe has a stellar reputation and..."

"Thank you," said Jimmie, hanging up the phone. He moved on to the next listing and hit the second number.

This time it was a recorded message. "You've reached the Law Offices of Coehill and Associates. If you know the extension of the person you are trying to reach, please enter it now. To browse the company directory, please press 1 now. Or, stay on the line, and someone will be with you shortly." Typical on-hold music played. After three minutes, a gruff female voice answered. "Coehill and Associates. How may I direct your call?"

"I'd like to speak with one of your senior attorneys, please."

"I'm afraid, sir, you'll need to be more specific. Tell me the nature of your call, and I can direct it to someone who may assist you."

"I've come into a large amount of money, and I need legal representation to help me protect my assets."

"Thank you, please hold." Again, the music. This time someone quickly answered the phone. "George Lyle."

"Mr. Lyle, I need help in protecting my financial assets. I've come into a large amount of money and need help with my long-term planning."

"We can do that. How much is large?"

"I'd rather not say."

"Ok. I'm sure I could assign your case to someone."

"I want one of your senior people on this."

"Unless you are willing to tell us the amount, we won't assign a senior person. We'll make that decision after we meet."

"Fair enough. I have another question. What do you think of Luther Monroe and the Monroe Group."

"I find your question to be inappropriate, and I refuse to answer on principle."

"Thank you." Jimmie hung up the phone. He dialled the next number. "Lucy Davidson, Attorney at Law."

"May I speak to Ms. Davidson, please?"

"Speaking."

"Oh. I came into a large amount of money, and I am looking for legal representation to help me with protecting my assets and in long-range planning."

"Ok. I'm looking at my calendar."

"What is your earliest available appointment?"

"I could squeeze you in this afternoon if that works for you?"

"It does. One question. What do you think of Luther Monroe and the Monroe Group?"

There wasn't even a pause. "I find Mr. Monroe's ethics to be suspect, and his firm is the type that gives lawyers a bad name."

"Great. You're hired. I can be in your office in twenty minutes if that is ok?"

"I'd need to move stuff around, but yes. You seem anxious."

"I am. I want to start right away."

"Ok. See you in twenty minutes." The line went dead.

Jimmie put the phone on the table, took one last drag on his cigarette and stubbed it out. Then he took a long drink. He contemplated going over to Chester's to tell his mother but decided against it. He wanted to get everything set up before anyone else knew.

Jimmie put on the suit Big Sonny had gotten for him. Now he felt like someone with money.

It took him nineteen minutes after the phone call with Lucy Davidson to get to her law office in a strip plaza. He opened up the door, and an electronic tone announced his entrance.

"I'll be right with you." He waited in the small lobby. An empty reception desk with no personal items on it, showing no one was using it, dominated the small space. There were two offices, a conference room and a copy room.

"Hi, there. I'm Lucy Davidson. You must be the gentleman who called? Everything happened so quick I forgot to get your name." She extended her hand to him.

Lucy was an attractive blond woman his age, maybe younger. She wore a navy skirt and matching blazer with a cream coloured blouse. She appeared to be very fit, at least that's the impression he got from seeing her calves.

"Jimmie Mayfield." He took her offered hand and gave it a shake.

"Come in. Sorry, but I'm short-staffed at the moment. My receptionist, well, it wasn't working out, and I haven't replaced her. So, I'm pulling double duty here. Why don't you come back to my office?"

"Ok."

The furniture was new and of excellent make. He glanced around at the things hanging on her walls—a picture of her in running gear, wearing a racing bib. A medal from the Walt Disney World Marathon hung around the picture frame. Another photo with a young woman at Machu Picchu, and a photo of the two holding hands in front of the Leaning Tower of Pisa. A third showed them sharing a tender kiss. A picture of her receiving her diploma and one of her, in her graduation gown, with the same young woman and an older version of Lucy. He pulled his eyes away from the pictures to see her law degree on the wall. Harvard Law School, summa cum laude, 2015.

"Please sit, Mr. Mayfield, and tell me how I can help you." She sat in her chair.

Jimmie sat in a chair across from her. He reached into his wallet, took out the ticket, smoothed it out and slid it across the desk towards her. She reached out for the ticket, curious. She picked it up, looked at it, and her eyes opened wide. "Is this...?"

The (Extra)ordinary Life of Jimmie Mayfield

"The winning ticket from last night's big lottery draw? The five hundred and twelve million dollars one? Yes. I need help deciding my next steps."

"We need to decide how you will accept this money."

"I'll take the lump sum over the annuity."

"So, you've done your homework. But I meant the specifics of the actual going to the lottery corporation to get the money. We should set up an LLC, that's a limited liability company..."

"Yes, I'm aware of what an LLC is. I'm a trained paralegal."

"Too bad for me you won this money, huh? I've been looking for one to join me here."

So, there were paralegal jobs available. But then he had five hundred and twelve million reminders of why he was here. He never needed to work for anyone again.

"I recommend you accept the money through your LLC. This will protect you personally. People will crawl out of the woodwork. Any earlier transgressions in your past or that occur in the next few months will come to the forefront. This should protect you from frivolous lawsuits since the money sits in the LLC, of which you will be the only shareholder. I would advise any significant purchases you make be made through the LLC, so the LLC keeps ownership of the assets, not Jimmie Mayfield."

"This is why I came to you."

"I should put you in touch with a financial planner. I can advise you on what you should do from a legal perspective but talk to someone specializing in this level of financial planning. Taxes need to be paid." She took out a calculator and punched in some numbers. "Rough guess, your five hundred and twelve million becomes three hundred and seventeen million, give or take if you take the lump sum."

"Ok, that's still quite a bit of money."

"But wait, there's more. The federal government withholds another twenty-five percent of your winnings. So that's..." more calculations. "That's another seventy-nine and a quarter million off the top. You're down to two hundred and thirty-seven million. They'll tax you at the highest rate...I know Congress has been talking about tax reform. Still, even if that gets passed, it won't kick in until next year, so you must pay another fourteen-point six percent to make up the remaining taxes not withheld." More calculations. "I'd estimate that once these deductions are applied, and the taxes paid, you'll end up with two hundred and three million dollars."

"It's funny, isn't it? If someone had told me yesterday, I'd win two hundred million dollars, I'd be overjoyed. But this morning, I thought I'd won over five hundred million, and you telling me it's now two hundred million, I'm less enthused."

"Uncle Sam wants his share."

"Yeah, but why is his share bigger than mine?"

Lucy laughed. "I don't know. Ask Congress why that is the case."

"I might do that."

"You must claim your prize at the Florida Lottery Headquarters in Tallahassee. You have sixty days after the draw to claim it; today is day one."

"I'm claiming it as soon as possible. I want the money by the end of the week."

"Ok, they will need to verify your identity. You'll either need a U.S. Passport, a U.S. Armed Forces ID Card or a card issued by the Bureau of Citizenship and Immigration Services. I assume you're a US citizen?"

"Born and bred right here in Englewood."

"Well, great, that means you have a Social Security number. If you didn't, they would withhold more. Now, if you don't have any of those forms of ID, a Florida state driver's license will do."

"That's good because I don't."

"Do you have a bank account?"

"No. I've never needed one. Nor a credit card."

"You don't own any property? A job that deposits your pay to an account? How did you cash your paycheque without an account?"

"I used those cheque-cashing places. I'm a simple guy who got lucky."

"But you said you were a paralegal?"

"I'm not currently practicing that profession."

"That's fine. I'm not here to judge. I'm here to represent you the best I can. So far, this has been off the clock, but you will need to sign a personal services agreement for me to act as your agent in this matter. We must get you set up at a bank with a bank account to wire transfer you the money. We can start and make travel arrangements to Tallahassee. You won't get this done today, so we can't leave for Tallahassee until tomorrow. Where do you plan to store the ticket until then?"

"I hadn't thought of it. I only found out I'd won an hour ago."

"I'd recommend finding a safe location, a safety deposit box, to store the ticket. There's a place with deposit boxes near here. Or, I have a fireproof safe on the premises if you are comfortable doing that? I'll only take possession on your behalf after you've signed the agreement. If you have any hesitation in leaving it here with me, I'd recommend you to get the safe deposit box."

Jimmie stared at her. "I think I can trust you."

"I'm glad to hear. Because it's only the beginning. Getting this set up and claiming the prize is the easy part. It will get harder from here." She leaned forward in her chair. "This will change your life, you know, in ways you haven't even contemplated. And not always for the best. Nothing will ever be the same."

"I know. I always said this was a sure way to ruin your life."

"Not if you're smart. And you're taking the right steps."

"I'll take it one day at a time."

"It's all any of us can do," said Lucy. She smiled and stood. "Let me get you that paperwork."

215

About the Author

Troy Young

Troy has been many things in his career. Shoe salesman, waiter, newspaper owner, children's performer, actor, elected official, policy adviser, CEO and university lecturer. Now he wants to try his hand at writing. Jimmie Mayfield's genesis came while going for a walk in Placida, Florida, where his parents have a winter home. Jimmie Mayfield is the first novel he wrote, but the third novel to be published.

When not exploring Florida, Troy lives in Toronto with his wife, daughter and dog.

Author Website: www.floridamanthenovel.com
Amazon Author Page: amazon.com/author/troyyoung
Twitter and Facebook: @FloridaNovel
Instagram: @troyyoung1971

Made in the USA
Columbia, SC
30 April 2022